About the author

Charlie Douglas Gutsell is twenty-four years old. He first fell in love with writing whilst completing his BA Honours in English Language. His love for the craft, and in particular both historical and fast paced action, only grew and he went on to complete a Masters in Creative Writing. He loves the escapism that stories offer the reader.

IN A VALLEY OF KINGS

Charlie Douglas Gutsell

IN A VALLEY OF KINGS

Vanguard Press

VANGUARD PAPERBACK

© Copyright 2021
**Charlie Douglas
Gutsell**

A CIP catalogue record for this title is
available from the British Library.

ISBN 978-1-80016-016-3

*Vanguard Press is an imprint of
Pegasus Elliot MacKenzie Publishers Ltd.*
www.pegasuspublishers.com

First Published in 2021

**Vanguard Press
Sheraton House Castle Park
Cambridge England**

Printed & Bound in Great Britain

Dedication

For Mum, Dad, Harry and Stacy.

Acknowledgements

I would like to thank my family and friends for their tireless support during the creation of this book.

Prologue
The Birth of a Legacy

The eighteenth dynasty has, and will, see numerous leaders which will incite much controversy throughout Egypt, but perhaps few will live up to the reign of a pharaoh determined to revolutionise the Egyptian culture forever. The Egyptian pharaoh, King Amenhotep III, was dead and his son, Amenhotep IV, was crowned as the new pharaoh of the empire. A believer in a sole deity, known as the Aten, Amenhotep IV would change his name to Akhenaten (roughly translated as he who is of service to the Aten) during the fifth year of his reign. A man who thought himself to be a descendent of God, Amenhotep IV was determined to cement his legacy as a true God to the Egyptian people. For too long he viewed that his people had been worshiping multiple deities, and he now felt that it was time for his culture to evolve. Egypt's supreme leader was attempting to rewrite their way of life, and their history forever.

1
Lessons
1346 B.C.

"Look up at the sky. Tell me what you see."

Young Dakarai looked up at the glistening sky.

"I see the stars, and just the dark." He looked at his father and smiled.

"Ha, close, but no. Look harder, son. Don't look with your eyes, look with your heart, and you'll see something much more." The gleaming stars and jet-black sky made Waset resemble something from another world, each star shining in a totally unique way, each teasing a different story that could ignite one's imagination. Dakarai squinted his eyes in an attempt to try and see what his father was talking about. He then tilted his head, but still nothing.

"Father, I can't see anything."

Akil leant down, now level with his son. He put his arm over Dakarai's shoulder and pointed to the sky.

"In time you'll learn, my son. The moon, the stars, the energy flowing around us, these are the work of the Gods. Whatever you see, touch, smell or hear, these are all gifts from our many Gods."

Young Dakarai stared at his father, eyes wide open,

with an innocent grin now beginning to appear on his face. He had never heard stories of such mystery and wonder before.

"Can they see us, Father?"

Akil smiled. "They can, my son. Everywhere you go, they will watch over you. When the time comes that I can no longer be by your side, I promise you that the Gods will watch over you, forever."

As Akil stood up, Dakarai looked up at his father, unsure what to make of that comment. "But Father, no one can kill you. You won't leave me. Never ever."

Akil looked down at his son and smiled in an attempt to mask what he was really thinking. "One day, Dakarai, everyone must leave this world and join the Gods up there in eternity. But don't you worry, my son, I'll still be keeping a close eye on you."

Dakarai put his arms around his father's waist and squeezed him tight.

"Come on, my two star gazers, come in for some food."

Answering the call of his mother, Dakarai turned around. Akil picked up his son, putting him over his shoulders, and the two of them headed back inside for their evening meal.

Living on the outskirts of Waset, their village rested neatly on top of a giant sand dune, providing an excellent view of the city, and in particular the pharaoh's palace. Consisting of only eight other families, it was a quaint, but tranquil community.

Situated far enough so to not aggravate the pharaoh, and yet not too far away that they would be cut off from the rest of civilisation, their village was positioned perfectly. In their view, they had an abundance of wealth.

Dakarai and his father sat down, as Lapis began to serve up their meal. Their home was not a palace by any means, but it suited their needs. Other than being a fisherman, Akil was a very creative individual. He and some of the others from the community had constructed all of the homes in the village. A single floor shack constructed from a combination of mud and stone, it may not have looked like much, but to the family it was home.

"So, what have my two favourite boys been doing on this fine evening?" Lapis, Dakarai's mother was the image of perfection. She was often considered by the villagers to be a human depiction of Hathor, the Goddess of beauty. Adored by all, none more so than her husband, Akil, Lapis was the one that truly made the abode that the family lived in to feel like a home.

"Father was teaching me about all of the Gods, Mother, and that they'll look after me once you're all dead."

Lapis dropped the pot she was holding. With her eyes wide open, she turned to Akil. "What are you doing? Have you no shame? Do you not realise what will happen if you continue this rebellion?"

Akil finished his mouthful before responding. "I

was showing our son the truth. The truth of our existence, and the truth of our destiny."

"Akil, we've spoken about this, you cannot go around, advocating the many Gods, by order of the pharaoh. I don't want to see you tried and killed for nothing but your own stubborn pride. And there's not a chance that you're dragging our son into this."

Dakarai never liked watching his parents argue. He used to run to his bed and tried to sleep through the argument. Things were different now though; he was eleven years old, and in his eyes, he was a young man, and he wanted to act as such.

"It's all right, Mother, I will not speak of this to anyone. This can just be our little secret."

Dakarai's Mother sighed, glanced at Akil, and then back to Dakarai. "You are a good boy, Dakarai, we just need to be careful. We don't want your father getting any of us into trouble."

Dakarai stood up straight in an attempt to look taller. "Don't worry, mother. I won't say anything, and even if that bad man did come, I'd protect you and Father, all by myself."

Both Akil and Lapis chuckled.

"We know you would, my boy. Now go on to bed, it's getting late," Akil said as Dakarai began to slowly make his way to bed.

Once Dakarai had gone to bed, Lapis and Akil finished cleaning their few pots and little cutlery. The two then sat outside, admiring their now starlit village.

"Forgive me, my love. I just have no wish to see you perish on the order of a madman."

Akil put his arm around Lapis. The two of them were looking up to the cosmos, observing its great mystique and beauty. Akil turned to his wife.

"Do not fear, my darling. I understand perfectly well the consequences of my actions. I will stop educating our neighbours with the truth, but I will not deny our son the right to know his identity."

Lapis pulled her husband in closer. "I just don't want to lose you."

Akil held his wife's hands. "I give you my word, as your husband and best friend, no harm shall come to us. And if our pharaoh sees fit to punish the spreading of truth, then let him be dragged down by Osiris himself."

Lapis smiled. "I love you, Akil."

"And I you, Lapis. And I you," Akil said, as he and his wife hugged each other one last time before going back inside for some rest.

2
The pharaoh
1346 B.C.

The sun had now set on the ancient city of Waset, with a full moon's gaze reflecting off of the pharaoh's palace, causing the countless jewels and golden decorations surrounding the outside of the structure to shine and glisten in the night. To the left of the palace, the pharaoh's falcon was flying around the perimeter of the palace, before making its way back into the pharaoh's chambers. Flying through an exposed window, the falcon landed on a perch next to the pharaoh's bed, a perch where it remained.

Having completed his business for the day, the pharaoh, now going by the name Akhenaten, had retired to his chambers, and was awaiting the arrival of his evening meal. Revolutionising one's culture was exhausting work, and the pharaoh was almost salivating at the mouth at the thought of being able to devour whatever creation the servants might bring to their ravenous king. The pharaoh's chambers were, much like the rest of his palace, a lavish, jewel laden example of what power and authority can offer one of status in ancient Egypt. The pharaoh was convinced that he was a descendent of God, and therefore wanted to be treated as such. Getting ever frustrated at having to wait for his meal, the pharaoh was in discussion with the Medjay general, Kek regarding his revolutionary plan, a plan that would cement his legacy.

"Report, General Kek, how is construction progressing?"

"With haste, my Pharaoh. We are working the men tirelessly to achieve your vision. Akhetaten will soon become the new capital, and the worship of the one true God can commence."

The pharaoh smiled, clenching his fists. "So it begins. This blasphemous age of multiple deities will soon be at an end, and the era of the Aten will truly be able to begin."

"My Pharaoh, we still need to address the many preachers throughout the kingdom who advocate the many Gods. When shall we deal with them?"

The pharaoh began to navigate his way through his chambers. "In time, General Kek. In time. All you are to do is keep a close watch on them. Let them think that we allow the spreading of blasphemy. When the time comes that they feel truly safe, then that is the time we will strike. For now, you and the rest of the Medjay will remain observant. Your time will come." The pharaoh then sat down.

The general too, now modelled a sinister grin as one of the pharaoh's servants swiftly came through into his chambers with a mouth-watering goose, decorated with numerous vegetables, with a second platter scattered with fresh fruit and nuts. Sweating heavily, his arms and knees shaking, the servant knew that he was late.

"My deepest apologies, my King. Your meal is served."

Both the pharaoh and General Kek glared at the servant, their stares like knives spearing through his head. The pharaoh stood up from his seat, now looking down on the servant.

"Let this happen again, and I assure you, the next time a meal comes through that door, it will be you that is being served."

"Of course, my Pharaoh. Once again, my deepest apologies, it will never happen again. Have a good evening, Lord Amenhotep."

The servant took a heavy gulp before making his way out of the pharaoh's chambers. However, as he began to leave the chambers, he was immediately stopped by General Kek, who grabbed his throat and slammed the servant against a wall.

"You dare address your pharaoh by that name?" As Kek squeezed ever tighter on the servant's throat, his face began to lose its natural colour and instead began to adopt a dark blue. The pharaoh slowly made his way over to Kek and the servant.

"It's okay, General, put him down. It was an honest mistake."

The general looked at the pharaoh, before releasing

his grip on the servant, causing him to hit the floor gasping for air. The pharaoh then sat next to the breathless servant, putting his arm over his shoulder.

"We all make mistakes, don't we? You failed to bring my food to me on time."

The servant began to get his breath back. His bloodshot eyes looked into the pharaoh's.

"And I have failed to rely on my servants to get the simple task of getting my name right. Oh well, no matter."

As the pharaoh patted the servant on the back, he pulled a long serrated, golden blade out from under his robe and steered it through the servant's jaw and up into his brain. Blood now squirting out of the servant's head from all angles, his body rolled onto the floor as the last remnants of life were sucked out from his now shell of a body. The pharaoh leant down so to whisper into the corpse's ear.

"Never again will you make such a multitude of mistakes. Never again will I be referred to by that name. I am a divine. I am a God. My name is Akhenaten."

The pharaoh turned to General Kek. "A change of plans is in order, General. I want you to find all of the preachers and traitors that infest my empire. I want you to find them all. We are going to wipe them out. All of them. Now go. Go!"

General Kek teased a dark smile, while beginning to leave the pharaoh's chambers. "With great pleasure, my Pharaoh."

The pharaoh then kicked the corpse that was now staining the floor. "And take this thing with you, it's ruining the floor."

3
Making an Example
1340 B.C.

As months turned into years, just as he was ordered, General Kek began to hunt down and dispose of all who dared to advocate the many gods, and in doing so, had disobeyed their Pharaoh. He was ruthless. Word spread like wildfire of Kek's mission, with every village from Waset to Akhetaten seeking refuge from Kek's devastation. The only village to stand firm in the wake of Kek's onslaught was a small village based just outside of Waset, on top of a large sand dune.

***

Dakarai had grown up to become a very mature young man. At seventeen he was now able to accompany his father on all of his fishing trips, as well as catching fish of his own. Dakarai was truly making his parents proud. Loving his life, Dakarai was in a state of true happiness. Little did he know, his world was about to come crashing down.

One afternoon, Dakarai was making his way down to the river, in order to speak with his father. He had just learned some news from the capital.

"Ii-ti, Mother. Where is Father? I need to speak with him."

Dakarai's mother was also outside. She was seeing to the horses. "Ii-ti, Mother. How are you this morning? Is there anything that I could help you with? Why don't you try that again, Dakarai?"

Dakarai sighed. "Forgive me, Mother, but I must make haste. There is something that I must discuss with Father."

Lapis pointed to the far side of the river. "He's over there, finishing the construction of his new net. Perhaps once you've spoken to him you can then help me to feed the cows?"

"Thank you, Mother." Dakarai made his way down to the far side of the river.

Lapis watched her son make his way before muttering under her breath, "Ah yes, and maybe Ra shall return to Earth in human form. In your dreams, Lapis."

As Dakarai wandered over to his father, he could see that Akil's new net was of a unique design. It was much like that of his traditional net, around six foot in length, and capable of catching around twenty fish. However, this net was seemingly attached to their papyrus raft, meaning that while the raft was in motion, the net could expand and catch fish without the need of too much human interference.

"Ah, at last. This will work perfectly," Akil

chuckled to himself.

As Dakarai walked over to his father, Akil was emptying the contents of the net. He had just caught a tasselled scorpionfish. Akil carefully picked up the fish using his net, and returned it to the water. Dakarai was left confused.

"Why would you do that?"

Akil turned to his son. "That fish is just like us, my son. He will have a family that loves and misses him. He swam into the net by accident, so it is not my decision of whether he lives or dies. That is for the Gods to decide. And besides, he is quite poisonous." Akil walked over to Dakarai and hugged him. "What can I do for you, my son?"

Dakarai hugged his father back. "I have news from the new capital. Work is complete, and Akhetaten is now officially Egypt's new centrepiece. The pharaoh decrees that the worship of the Aten will truly begin."

Akil laughed. "Wonderful. Now far away from us, all that is left is for our noble pharaoh to finally decide what his name is. He is beginning to go by more names than the Gods, themselves. I suppose that will also mean that he can raise that new son of his far away from us. What was his name again?" Akil chuckled once more, but Dakarai remained unmoved by his father's joke.

"His name is Tutankhamen. Anyway, that does not matter right now. There is something else, Father."

Akil turned away, walking back towards his fishing net. "Are you talking about the Medjay general?"

Dakarai walked over to his father. "You've heard?"

"I heard the elders discussing it this morning. Let him come, he will not strike fear into this village. We are a strong people. He will not intimidate us into submission."

The unease in Dakarai's voice began to increase. "Have you not heard the stories, Father? He has been butchering Egyptian citizens all over the land. Those who preach of the many Gods. Those like you."

Akil turned to Dakarai, and put his arm over his son's shoulder. "I assure you, my son, there are no men like me." Akil looked at Dakarai, eye-to-eye and smiled. Akil had always been a confident, yet humble man who thought that he could take on the world. But this was a problem much larger than himself, and Dakarai's concern regarding his father's stubbornness was growing.

"Father, I don't think you understand. What we do in the comfort of our own homes is our business, but you're still preaching to the village. Even after you promised Mother you'd stop, all those years ago. You're showcasing yourself to the rest of Egypt, and it'll be just a matter of time before that Medjay general comes to stop you." Dakarai pointed to his mother, and the rest of the villagers. "Look at what we have, Father. It may not be the wealth and riches that the pharaoh possesses in Akhetaten, but this is our home, and I for one have no desire to lose it."

Akil sighed, looked to the ground, and then back at

Dakarai. "Maybe you're right, my son. But how can I deny these people, our friends, the truth? They'd be living a lie, and that is something that cannot be allowed to stand. I have a duty as a child of the Gods to share their wisdom."

Dakarai was left stunned at his father's attitude regarding the severity of their situation. Akil had always been a stubborn individual, but it appeared that the ageing fisherman was not comprehending the position that the family was in.

"Father, you know we support each other in everything we do, but this is madness."

Akil smiled at his son once more. "Trust me, my son. I know what I'm doing."

Dakarai, with hands on his hips, muttered under his breath at the sheer frustration at not being able to change his father's mind. Akil chucked at his son's annoyance.

Dakarai then suddenly paused for a moment, as the ground began to lightly vibrate under his feet. He could hear what sounded like a group of horses galloping towards him. "Can you hear that, Father? I thought all of the horses were accounted for?"

Akil put his hands over Dakarai's shoulders. "They can wait. You know, you remind me more and more of your mother every day."

Dakarai, unsure what to make of that, tilted his head. "And do you plan on criticising that?"

Akil pulled Dakarai in close and touched his son's heart. "No. Being able to see your mother in you makes

27

this old fisherman so very proud. You are growing up to be a greater man than I could ever hope to be, and your mother and I cherish you every day. Will you promise me one thing?"

Dakarai looked into his father's eyes. A tear was rolling down Akil's cheek.

"Never change, Dakarai. Never change." Akil pulled his son in close, and the two of them exchanged the sincerest of heartfelt embraces. Despite the impending danger that had Dakarai so concerned, while embracing his father, for a brief moment at least, Dakarai seemed to forget the reason that caused him to feel so frustrated in the first place. Despite all of the uncertainty and concern regarding Akhenaten's plans, for this one brief instant it did not seem to bother Dakarai. He was enjoying the company of his father. Akil then let go of his son.

"Come on. Let us prepare the nets for this evening."

As Dakarai followed his father to set up the nets, the galloping sound began to get louder. If these were a group of horses, then they were getting closer. Dakarai wandered away from the river to get a better view. With desperate terror now filling his body, Dakarai saw a group of five Egyptian soldiers carrying the pharaoh's colours and riding towards their village. They were being led by General Kek. The reckoning had arrived. With his breath quickened and his pulse racing, Dakarai sprinted back towards the river where his father remained totally oblivious.

With Dakarai seemingly gone for longer than he had envisioned, Akil began to wonder where his son had disappeared to. Wandering just a few metres away from the water's edge, Akil began to call out to his son.

"Dakarai, where have you run off to?" With the sun's rays spearing down, impeding the old man's vision, Akil finally began to make out what appeared to look like a figure running towards him. Accompanying the figure was a faint noise, that began to slowly become clearer and more intelligible the closer the figure became.

"Father, run. Go!"

Just as Akil finally began to notice that it was his son sprinting towards him, a group of five jet-black stallions raced past Dakarai, just narrowly avoiding him. As they mercilessly tore their way down towards the river, it was clear that Akil was their intended target. Reaching the edge of the river, and with devastating efficiency, the soldiers began to circle the old fisherman. All Akil could do was stand firm, modelling whatever bravery he'd managed to exert from each and every fibre of his being. For he was surrounded.

With the soldiers now blocking any chance of escape, the horses remained static. Each soldier stared down at Akil, menacingly. Looking at the horse directly in front of him, Akil watched as the soldier swiftly dismounted and slowly began to walk towards him. In his golden robes, the soldier's large frame nearly shielded Akil's entire body from the sun. Despite having never met him before, Akil knew that he was about to come face to face with General Kek.

"You are the one known as Akil?"

Dropping his net, Akil simply nodded his head. Even with his heart racing, he was the picture of composure. "I am."

Kek smiled. "Do you know why we are here?"

Akil glanced around at the soldiers. Turning back to Kek, he too offered a smile. "You're here to silence the spreading of truth. But you won't. The truth will always prevail."

Stepping forward, Kek stood just an arm's length from Akil. With him stood so close, Akil could feel the heat coming off of him.

"We are agents of the pharaoh himself, and we are here to end your reign of blasphemy."

With Kek still glaring down at him, out of the corner of his eye Akil once more noticed his son, only now, he was much closer, but still sprinting towards him. This caused his pulse to quicken even more. He glanced back up at Kek, meeting the bigger man's gaze.

"What are you going to do?"

While chuckling to himself, but at the same time seemingly gritting his teeth, Kek's eyes widened. "Whatever I see fit." With one swift motion, Kek drew his sword and pointed it directly at Akil's throat. The sun's rays reflected off of the sword's tip, causing Akil's vision to be somewhat impaired. Glancing down at the sword, and then up towards Dakarai who was still sprinting towards him, Akil smiled.

"Whatever you do, whatever evil you rain down on my people, will mean nothing when the Gods serve justice on you, and your pharaoh."

With his muscles tensing, and his eyes widened, Kek drew back his sword. "I am justice. May your Gods show you mercy." With one devastatingly smooth stroke, Kek steered his blade straight through Akil's neck, causing the old man to collapse, dead before he even hit the floor.

Feeling like he'd been punched in the stomach, Dakarai stopped dead in his tracks, capable of no words other than a heartbroken scream. Unaware of his presence, Kek turned around, following the noise, to see Dakarai standing alone. He offered a victorious smirk that proved the only explanation for his actions, and he reeked of victory. He pointed towards Dakarai.

"Two of you take the boy. The rest of you... destroy the village."

As two of the soldiers began to ride straight for Dakarai, the others followed the general down towards the village. Unable to save his father, Dakarai knew that he'd be no use to anyone if he was dead. Turning back the way he'd come, he ran back up the sand dune in search of refuge. As he reached the top, Dakarai could make out what looked like an abandoned pyramid; one that may have been part of a previous dynasty. With nothing else for as far as the eye could see, Dakarai headed for the pyramid.

As he stood outside its entrance, Dakarai quickly scaled the giant structure with his eyes. With tears still streaming down his face, he noticed that some of the stones at the pyramid's base had begun to crack and had become loose; most likely from years of erosion. Beginning to hear the clattering hooves of the soldier's horses, Dakarai knew that it was now or never. Pushing out the loose stones one by one, he'd managed to create a wide enough gap that he could slip through into the pyramid. Jumping through the gap, Dakarai managed to cover it back up with other, smaller stones that were scattered on the ground around him. He was at last hidden.

Reaching the top of the sand dune, not more than twenty metres away from the pyramid, the soldiers looked out into the distance. With nothing but a viciously thick heatwave in front of them, Dakarai was nowhere to be seen. Turning to one another, they both wiped the sweat dripping from their forehead.

"The boy is gone. Let him run. The desert will consume him now."

The other soldier nodded, still getting his breath back.

"Yes. We should return to the village, or at least what's left of it. Come, I can already smell the flames of justice."

With the taste of smoke already beginning to stain the soldiers' teeth, the two of them headed down the sand dune, back towards the village. With the soldiers now gone, and with his friends and family all being attacked in the village, Dakarai hid inside the pyramid, terrified. Alone and terrified.

4
The Promise
1340 B.C.

Taking long, stuttering breaths, Dakarai's face continued to flood with tears. Pushing his palms up against his eyes, he finally managed to stop the tears. Taking a deep breath, Dakarai began to navigate his way through the pyramid. Scaling the inside of the poorly lit structure with his eyes, Dakarai was left in awe as he looked around at the tattooed walls of the pyramid. Giant sets of hieroglyphics and paintings depicted Dakarai's ancient ancestors bowing and praying before the many Egyptian deities. Looking up at these structures, Dakarai couldn't help but think back to many years ago.

"In time you'll learn, my son. The moon, the stars, the energy flowing around us, these are the work of the Gods. Whatever you see, touch, smell or hear, these are all gifts from our many Gods."

Thinking back to that time of such innocence and wonder, it had been many years since Dakarai was greeted with these emotions. Even in a time of such darkness, it was nice to feel something positive again.

As the minutes continued to pass, Dakarai knew

that it was time to make his way back to the village. Moving the stones he'd used to hide himself away, Dakarai left the pyramid. As soon as he found himself outside, the stench of thick smoke began to fill his lungs. Something was very wrong. Making his way back down the sand dune, Dakarai stood in horror as he stared down at a real-life depiction of Hell itself. His village was up in flames. Wiping the tears from his eyes, Dakarai sprinted down the sand dune. The village needed his help.

Arriving at his village, Dakarai was forced to duck and dodge the flames that were engulfing his home. There was only one thought going through his mind... get home. As he finally made it, Dakarai could only stare in shock to see his family home burning to the ground.

"Mother!"

With no answer, Dakarai was left with only one choice. He had to go inside himself. Fighting his way through the flames that were showing absolutely no mercy, Dakarai was left with the unforgiving sight of his mother, laying deadly still on the ground. She was burnt to a crisp. Amongst the roaring flames and crashing rubble, Dakarai dropped to his knees.

"Mother, no!"

Resentfully accepting that she was dead, Dakarai simply kissed his mother on the forehead, and then quickly carried her corpse out of the shack, which was swiftly collapsing to the ground. As he carefully rested his mother down, outside the shack, Dakarai turned and could only watch as his childhood home was destroyed, the merciless flames showing the same brutality as the Medjay soldiers that caused them. With tears once more streaming down his face, Dakarai began to look around at the remainder of his village. His home was not the only one to suffer the same fate. With his village left to nothing but ashes, Dakarai looked over at the river, where his father still laid. As his eyes widened, he sprinted over to him. Perhaps there was still hope.

As he approached the river, any dwindling hope that he may have been clinging to had instantly vanished. Arriving at the river, he was greeted by the body of his father. With a pool of blood drenching his body, it was clear that Akil was long dead. Dropping to his knees, Dakarai cradled his father's head in his arms. Pressing his head up against his father's, Dakarai's tears were now uncontrollable.

"I'm sorry, Father. I'm so sorry. I love you. I love you, Father."

Akil's eyes were open, appearing to blindly stare into his son's. With a swift yet calm motion, Dakarai closed his father's eyes for the final time. Leaning down, he then kissed him on the forehead. It was time for Dakarai to finally let go. He was now on his own.

With the fire having at last calmed down, smoke continued to fill the air. As the evening breeze began to slowly greet a somewhat pleasant evening, the fumes began to shoot around and twist in the air in a seemingly majestic dance. It was almost hypnotic. Down below, with the damage caused by the fire on clear display throughout the remainder of the village, Dakarai was standing over a pair of freshly dug graves. As he kissed his palm and then placed it on both of the graves, Dakarai knew that he'd never feel the physical embrace of his parents again. Whilst being leant down on one knee in between the two graves, Dakarai bowed his head.

"I promise you, I will take your knowledge, your love, and your teachings. I will take them, and bring peace and prosperity back to Egypt." With tears still running down his face, Dakarai wiped them from his eyes.

"No more will our people be forced to live in fear of a pharaoh with care for no one but himself. The age of peace will return. The love for the Gods will continue. I swear to you both, I am going to end this." Once more kissing his palm and placing it on the graves, Dakarai stood to his feet. With his home destroyed and his family butchered, there was nothing left for him here anymore. It was time to exact vengeance. Looking out towards the almost endless desert that lay in front of him, Dakarai knew that somewhere out there was Akhetaten. Somewhere out there was the man responsible. With nothing on his person other than the rags on his back, Dakarai set out on his quest. His quest for Akhetaten. His quest for the pharaoh. His quest for revenge.

5
Victory
1340 B.C.

Akhetaten. Taking inspiration from his former home in Waset, the pharaoh had transformed the new capital into a haven, designed to celebrate the rule of the one true Egyptian idol, the Aten. His palace was as lavish and outrageous as ever. As the beating sun shone over the countless jewels that formed layer after layer, coating the outside of the palace, the consequential reflection was enough to blind any nearby birds that dared to fly over it.

Inside his palace, Akhenaten was simply sitting in his chambers, looking out at his ever-increasing empire. His look was as dominating as it was smug. For he was the Aten's vessel, and he was all powerful. His peaceful watch could not last long however, as he began to hear footsteps heading towards him, footsteps that sounded very familiar. With blood dripping from his sword onto the golden floor, General Kek removed his sword from its scabbard and kneeled before his king in the centre of the chambers. With Akhenaten's back still turned, Kek presented him with his blood-stained sword.

"The last of the traitors have been dealt with, my

Pharaoh."

Music to his ears, Akhenaten slowly turned around, and made his way over to General Kek. With Kek still bowed, presenting the sword, the pharaoh placed his hand over Kek's shoulder. Although he remained a picture of sobriety, inside Akhenaten was drunk with victory.

"It is over then. You have now brought peace and order to my empire. You are a hero, General Kek." With blood still dripping from its tip, Akhenaten took the sword and placed it on a nearby table. Making his way back over to the general, Akhenaten gestured that Kek stand to his feet.

"Rise, General. Ensure my kingdom remains the most feared in all the world. Go down to the armoury on your way out. You will receive an upgrade on your weaponry."

Standing to his feet, Kek bowed once more before his pharaoh.

"You are most generous, my Pharaoh. Thank you."

As the general made his way out of the chambers, Akhenaten made his way back over towards his balcony, where he could once more look out over his kingdom. Flying through the balcony and perching on the pharaoh's shoulder, his falcon now too, gazed out at the seemingly endless empire that its master controlled. With a giant, sinister grin on his face, Akhenaten now knew the full extent of his power. With his enemies vanquished, he was now invincible. Glancing up at the sky, a single tear rolled down his cheek.

"My legacy will be eternal. At long last, I am truly a God."

6
Kidnapped
1340 B.C.

The endless Egyptian desert served as nothing but mocking torment as Dakarai continued his journey towards Akhetaten. In truth, he did not even know if he was travelling in the right direction. With his breathing heavy and sweat dripping from his forehead, the sun's beating rays felt like Dakarai was carrying a gargantuan weight on his back. With no food or water to replenish his strength, he was growing ever weaker with each and every step. With the infernal heat that was beating down on him proving too much to take, Dakarai fell to his knees. Too weak to get up, he began to pass out. With his eyes growing heavier and heavier, Dakarai began to make out what looked like a pair of figures walking towards him. Unable to shout out, he could only whisper.

"Mother. Father."

As his eyes finally closed, the two figures approached. Two young men, one of a small, skinny build, and the other, in stark contrast was a much more robust, larger companion. Standing over Dakarai, they both looked somewhat confused at what they had found.

"Look here, Bast. It's a boy. A young boy."

Bast, the larger member of the two, nodded his head. He had a relieved smile on his face.

"Fantastic, Abrax. Get a fire going. I'm starving."

As Bast rushed towards Dakarai's body, Abrax, alarmed by his friend's intentions, jumped in between the two of them, refusing to let Bast pass.

"What are you thinking? Do not take another step. The Gods will punish you to a lifetime of damnation if you even consider eating that boy."

Not at all fazed by Abrax's warning, Bast simply shrugged his shoulders. "But I'm hungry. What are we even going to do with him?"

Rolling his eyes in frustration, Abrax pointed towards the east. "We have to help him. He'll die out here on his own. We have to take him back with us." Making his way over to Dakarai, Abrax took the boy's arms. He then gestured towards his legs. "Come on, help me. Take his legs."

Not accustomed to manual labour, or any labour for that matter, Bast sighed in frustration. "Fine."

Picking up Dakarai's legs, the two friends then began to carry him towards their home. Across the desert stood a small village, a village that also had suffered the oppression of the pharaoh, and a village that had, too, considered the idea of fighting back. Although he did not know it yet, Dakarai was on his way to a village that would change his life forever.

7
The al-Minya Refuge
1340 B.C.

Al-Minya. A small trading village. Despite trade being its primary vocation, this was a poverty-stricken place. With beggars scattered around the streets, and the Medjay keeping a very strict order, al-Minya optimised what every village looked like across the empire. Akhenaten's grip was vice-like, with not a single member of the empire free from his oppression.

Arriving into the centre of the village, Abrax and Bast were still carrying Dakarai. With the two of them both sweating heavily from their travels, Bast glanced down at Dakarai's legs, causing his right eye to twitch slightly. He then glanced up at his friend.

"Abrax, I don't think I'll make it. Can I just take one of his legs? I'm sure he'll be fine."

Looking back at Bast, Abrax simply glared at him. "No. You are not to harm him in any way. We must get him to the refuge."

The two of them continued to carry Dakarai through the streets of the village's bazaar. As they continued to try and stay cool, the streets were dominated by the town's seemingly countless merchants.

Selling spices and beads from every corner of the globe, the bazaar was filled with many different sights and smells that could both ignite one's senses and spark one's intrigue. Although a very poor area, when the Medjay were otherwise occupied and unable to keep watch, al-Minya was full of life. As they continued to wander through the streets, eventually the shade began to run out, and the sun returned, continuing to beat down on their backs. As they neared the refuge, a strong beam of sunlight shot over Dakarai's face, causing him to groan and begin to regain himself. Slightly opening his eyes, Dakarai began to laboriously turn his head in order to get a better sense of where he was. Glancing his head back, he noticed his legs moving through the air. Shaking his head, Dakarai thought he was stuck in a dream, but as his eyes continued to scale upwards, he noticed that a large man was carrying his legs. Meeting Dakarai's gaze, Bast's eyebrows rose.

"Er, Abrax?"

Realising that he was being carried by a pair of strangers, Dakarai's eyes shot fully open. He began squirming around, trying to free himself from their grasp. His squirms caused both Abrax and Bast to drop him to the ground. Now free from their clutches, Dakarai jumped to his feet, and with what little strength he had left, sprinted off into the al-Minya bazaar. Stunned, Abrax looked towards his friend, pointing at Dakarai.

"Come on. We need to get him."

Although not as quick as Dakarai, Abrax and Bast set off to catch him, and in doing so initiated a chase through the al-Minya streets.

Continuing to sprint through the streets, Dakarai was having to be at his most agile in order to slip past and dodge the sea of people that filled the streets. Glancing behind him, Dakarai checked to see the whereabouts of his pursuers.

"Get away from me."

Right behind Dakarai, Abrax and Bast continued their pursuit. Abrax called out to him. "Wait. Please stop running. We're only trying to help you."

Continuing to look back, it was clear that Dakarai had no intention of stopping. "I don't need your help. Leave me alone."

Despite being able to keep pace with Dakarai, Abrax was forced to slow down in order to allow Bast to catch up as he was falling behind.

"Bast, keep moving. We can't let him get away."

Pushing himself to the limit but now breathing very heavily, Bast was struggling. "I'm trying, Abrax. He's really fast."

With Abrax trying to keep Bast up with the pace, Dakarai was finally able to distance himself from the two of them. Needing to disappear from sight, he turned to run down one of the backstreets. Managing to run halfway down the backstreet, he was forced to stop as a young girl jumped into his way, blocking his path. With no way past her, and his pursuers beginning to catch up, his patience was wearing thin.

"Please let me pass."

Glancing up at Dakarai, into his eyes, the girl simply smiled at him, before suddenly punching him in the face with great force, a punch so hard that it knocked him out cold. As his body once more collapsed to the floor, Abrax turned into the backstreet and ran over to Dakarai and the girl. He was panting heavily. As he began to catch his breath, Abrax looked across at the girl and smiled.

"I was wondering when you were going to show up. Thank you, Chione."

Chione pointed at Dakarai's body, before leaning down so to pick him up. "Help me get him up. We need to get him to the refuge."

As Abrax began to help Chione pick Dakarai up, Bast turned into the backstreet, and jogged over towards them. With the sweat dripping down his face epitomising his dislike of physical labour, he too teased a mild smile when seeing Chione.

"Chione. Thank the Gods you were here. He was really fast."

Chione began to chuckle. "It's okay, Bast. Help us carry him to the refuge."

As Bast made his way over so to assist his two friends, Abrax turned to Chione. "How did you know he was with us, Chione?"

Chione glanced up at Abrax. "I heard rumours that

Kek had destroyed the village by the Waset river. I knew you two were near there, so I followed you. And when you made it back here, I tracked you so I knew that this boy would make it to the refuge alive."

Surprised that they had been followed during their trek to Waset, both Abrax and Bast turned to each other in shock, before turning back to Chione.

"W-w-we had no idea you were watching us."

Chione smiled. "You should know by now, I'm good at hiding in plain sight. Now come on, let's get this one to the refuge."

As the three of them all helped to pick Dakarai up, they began to head towards the refuge on the other side of the bazaar. Hidden away from the suspicious eyes of the Medjay, the refuge was built down one of the backstreets. With little light and no neighbouring homes, the refuge was disguised well. A small shack with no windows and a sealed door, from the outside it looked totally uninhabited. The best form of disguise.

Arriving at the refuge entrance, Abrax and Bast were carrying Dakarai, who was still knocked out. Chione cautiously walked up to the entrance. She knocked four times. A voice began to sound on the other side of the door.

"Hail to the sky."

Chione took a breath. "Hail, Amun."

The door swiftly opened and Chione wandered inside. The door closed behind her. Next up was Abrax, who walked up to the door. Bast was now carrying

Dakarai on his own. Abrax, just like Chione, knocked four times. The voice returned. "Hail to creation."

Abrax took a breath. "Hail, Ptah."

The door opened once more, with Abrax wandering inside. Just as before, the door closed behind him. Placing Dakarai over his shoulder, Bast then also knocked on the door four times.

"Hail to beauty."

He took a breath. "Hail, Hathor."

As the door swung open, Bast carried Dakarai inside, with the door closing behind him. They were at last inside the refuge.

8
Former Paradise
1340 B.C.

Wandering into the refuge, Bast still carried Dakarai over his shoulder. Standing in front of him was the voice from the other side of the door. Pilis, a tall man; slightly older than the rest, and the leader of the refuge, glanced over Bast's shoulder to see Dakarai, still out cold. Startled, Pilis glared at Bast. "Wait. Stop. Who is this?"

Bast sighed. "Not a meal. I can tell you that much."

Turning around, Chione looked to shed some light on their new guest.

"He's from the Waset river. His village was destroyed by Kek and the Royal Guard. He needs our help."

Sceptical towards their guest's intentions, Pilis squinted his eyes as he examined Dakarai's body. After a few seconds of inspection, he glanced at Chione and nodded his head.

"Okay then. Take him through into the main living quarters."

Chione smiled at Pilis as Bast carried Dakarai through into the living quarters. Placing him onto the nearest table, Chione, Bast, Abrax, Pilis, and anyone else present in the living quarters all crowded around Dakarai. They were not accustomed to outsiders being welcomed into the refuge. Meanwhile, Pilis went and filled a small bowl with some water. Pushing his way through the small crowd surrounding Dakarai, Pilis held the bowl over his head.

"Stand back."

As the crowd surrounding Dakarai each took a step back, Pilis poured the bowl of water all over his face. The shock of the cold water hitting his face caused him to wake up, coughing heavily. As the coughing began to calm down, Dakarai was able to regain himself. After taking a few deep breaths, he glanced around the room. With many different sets of eyes all focused on him, Dakarai was startled. His eyes began darting rapidly around the room as he looked for an escape route, but there was none.

"Who are you? What do you want from me?"

Looking rather guilty, Bast stepped forward. His arms were by his side. "We weren't going to eat you."

Shaking her head, Chione stepped in front of her friend. "You're from the Waset river, aren't you? Your village was attacked by the Medjay."

Dropping his head in sadness, a single tear rolled down Dakarai's cheek. "Kek and his men butchered my village. They left it in a pile of ash. And my parents…"

Already knowing what he was about to say, Chione placed her arm over Dakarai's shoulder. She sighed. "It's okay. You don't have to say any more. We already know the rest."

Dakarai began to take a few more deep breaths in order to compose himself. On the other side of the table, Abrax stepped forward. "We saw what happened to your village. We didn't think any of you survived. That's why when Bast and I found you, we wanted to bring you here. We had no intention to harm you. Although, Bast did want to eat you briefly."

Startled by that revelation, Dakarai turned to Bast, looking rather concerned. Bast quickly dropped his head. "Apologies."

Dakarai then glanced back at Chione, who stepped forward. "You're not the only one who's been affected by the pharaoh's madness."

Dakarai began to look around at the lost souls who sought refuge here in al-Minya. It was at that moment that he realised he was not alone. There were many others just like him. These people had their lives ripped apart and reduced to nothing more but brief memories that would one day be forgotten.

"Each of us have paid the heaviest prices in the pharaoh's pursuit of terror."

Continuing to look around, Dakarai then looked back towards Chione. He sighed and took a breath. "You've all lost someone close to you. I'm so sorry. We need to act. We must bring an end to the pharaoh's reign of destruction."

As everyone surrounding him each began to sigh to themselves, Pilis stepped away from the table, while

Chione once more placed her palm on Dakarai's shoulder.

"It's not as easy as that."

As Dakarai tilted his head, Pilis stepped forward. "The pharaoh thinks he's a God. Why do you think he changed his name to Akhenaten? He worships the sun disk and only the sun disk. He's been entrenched in this lie for so long now that he's managed to convince himself of this supernatural nobility. At this point he's basically untouchable."

Sitting up fully, Dakarai shook his head and jumped off of the table. Bast and Abrax quickly put out their arms so to catch him if he fell.

"Careful. You're still quite weak. Be careful."

Dakarai glanced at Abrax and smiled. "I'll be fine."

After pausing for a brief moment in order to maintain his balance, Dakarai, with his fists clenched, stormed up towards Pilis. "Then we must break through his armour. I promised my parents that I'd bring him to justice, and I'm not going back on that promise."

Turning his back on Dakarai, Pilis offered little more than a frustrated moan. "Oh, you fed a pair of corpses nothing but fantasies."

Clenching his fists even harder, Dakarai's eyes widened. "Don't you dare say that about my parents." Enraged, Dakarai lunged forward, looking to take down Pilis. However, just before he was able to get his hands on him, Bast grabbed his arms, holding him back.

"Calm yourself."

With Bast gripping his arms, Dakarai was forced to calm himself. As his breaths became steadier, Bast let go of him. Now free, Dakarai calmly walked up to Pilis, although his fists were still clenched. Pilis was glaring at him as he approached.

"You're not the first to make that promise, and you won't be the last." Pilis then pointed to everyone still present in the room. "Over the last few years, the pharaoh, Kek and the entire regime have destroyed our lives. And you don't think we all wanted vengeance? Of course we did. We are nothing compared to the forces at Akhetaten. There's nothing we can do." With nothing more to add, Pilis simply turned around and began to leave the living quarters. "You are welcome to stay here as long as you need. I'd advise you to get some rest, and clear your mind of thoughts of suicidal vengeance."

As Pilis then left the quarters, Dakarai just stood there, with his head lowered. In an effort to comfort him, Abrax made his way over. He placed his hand over Dakarai's shoulder. "I think it's time that you had something to eat."

With his head still dropped, Dakarai's eyes glanced up at Abrax. "How can he say that? We have a duty to our families, our ancestors." Lifting his head, Dakarai then looked at Abrax, and then over to Bast and Chione. A rare smile began to fill his face. "Thank you for taking me in. I'm sorry about our earlier troubles. It all just came as a bit of a shock to me. Anyway, we haven't been properly introduced. My name is Dakarai."

As everyone began to step forward, Abrax began pointing at each of them individually. "Right, yes, you're right. Well, I'm Abrax." He then pointed over towards Bast. "That's Bast."

Bast then waved over at Dakarai. "Sorry I wanted to eat you."

Dakarai chuckled as Abrax then pointed towards Chione.

"You've now met Pilis, so over here is—"

Chione stepped forward. "I'm Chione."

As Dakarai looked over at Chione, his eyes began to widen with his jaw dropping slightly. As he took some time to look at her, he realised that he'd never seen a creature like her before in his entire life. Her beauty left him totally starstruck. Her tanned skin and jet-black hair caused the hairs on Dakarai's arms to stand on end. He had to get closer to her. He had to talk to her. As he began to approach her, sweat began dripping down his forehead. However, before he could reach her, he felt Bast's giant hands grabbing his shoulders, and then spinning him around.

"It's time we got some food."

As Dakarai looked around, he saw everyone leaving the living quarters and heading through towards the hall. He sighed, but out of the corner of his eye, noticed Chione also heading for the hall. All was not lost after all. Following her, Dakarai too, made his way towards the hall.

The hall was a much longer room than the living

quarters. Inside there were two long tables which covered the entire room. Pilis, and the other refuge inhabitants were sitting on one table, while Dakarai, Bast, Abrax and Chione sat on the other. With food being a scarce luxury during these dark times, a bowl of lentils was all that was on offer. Still, given how starving Dakarai was, this felt like a feast. With Bast true to his word, he was eating very quickly. Dakarai though, despite being smaller, was keeping up with Bast. His hunger was on display for all to see. Watching his apparent lack of table manners, Chione chuckled, and placed her hand on Dakarai's arm.

"Hungry, are we?"

Glancing up at Chione, Dakarai paused for a moment in embarrassment. He then quickly swallowed his mouthful and wiped his face. He too chuckled. "Sorry, it's just been a while since I've eaten anything."

Chione smiled. "It's okay. I bet you're starving." Looking across at Bast, she wasn't impressed to see Bast continuing to scoff his meal down. She coughed in an effort to get Bast's attention. "At least Dakarai has an excuse to eat like that."

Bast wiped his face and then glanced over at Chione. "I can't help it if I'm hungry."

As Bast sank his face back into his bowl, he continued devouring his meal. Abrax then turned to Dakarai. He leaned in closer.

"So, the Waset river. It must be a beautiful place. All that sun, and the crystal-clear water. It sounds like utopia."

As Dakarai's eating began to slow dramatically, he glanced over at Abrax, teasing a smile. "It was paradise. The sand was perfectly smooth; enough so our animals were comfortable. Mother would see to them every morning and evening. They loved seeing her. And Father could take his raft on to the water. The water was so calm it often looked like Father was floating in mid-air."

As a tear began to roll down Dakarai's cheek, he quickly wiped his eyes. As he took a deep breath, Abrax glanced at Bast.

"He was always attaching contraptions to that raft. After a while it began to look like something from another world. Ha, ha. Yes, it was more than special. It was home. And now it's gone. Because of that monster.

As Dakarai wiped his eyes once more, everyone sat around the table each bowed their heads. Dakarai then took another breath as he continued composing himself.

"Why does the pharaoh, our ruler behave like this? Why does he despise our ancient heritage so much?"

9
The Price of Disobedience
1340 B.C.

Outside the pharaoh's Akhetaten palace, the sun was scorching. High in the sky and surrounded by no clouds, it was a truly glorious day. Standing alone high up in the balcony of his palace, Akhenaten was glaring down at the hundreds of citizens his Medjay soldiers had rounded up. With the streets completely crowded, everyone was being watched and surrounded by the Medjay. They were keeping the citizens penned in like chickens to the slaughter. There was one citizen, however, that was not packed in with the rest. Being held at the front of the gathering by General Kek, a lone Egyptian man was pushed forward, causing him to fall to the floor. As the man stood up, one could see that he was covered in chains, trapped. Standing high up on his balcony, Akhenaten simply lifted his hand in the air, and the entirety of the masses fell absolutely silent. He then stepped forward.

"Good people of the empire, I stand before you today, a disappointed pharaoh."

Akhenaten then pointed to the man in chains. As Kek then punched him in the chest, he fell to the ground once more. The pharaoh's finger remained pointed towards him.

"This man has been breaching the one rule which I hold dearest to my heart. Please tell the people what you have done."

The man looked up at Akhenaten, but remained defiantly silent, causing Kek to punch him again, harder than previously.

"Answer your pharaoh."

After once again hitting the floor, the man laboriously made his way to his feet. He looked up at the pharaoh and took a deep breath.

"I was telling stories of our Gods, our heritage, and our destiny. You can't take these away from us. No matter what evil you bring to this land, the Gods will save us."

Taking a moment to simply glare at this disobedient Egyptian, Akhenaten glanced over at Kek and nodded, causing the general to light a block of wood. Kek then launched the block straight at the man, which caused him to catch fire. With the flames spreading all over his body in mere seconds, he was burning alive. As the man dropped to the floor, squirming and screaming, the potent stench of his skin beginning to bubble and melt away could be smelt by all. Looking on with great intensity, the pharaoh felt emotionally aroused at being able to demonstrate this kind of power to his subjects. With Akhenaten looking on, General Kek simply watched the man dying right in front of him, smiling as he did. As the squirming finally stopped and his screams went mute, the motionless corpse of the defiant man simply laid there on the ground. He was dead. As the masses all gathered round the body could only look on in terror, Akhenaten, looking over at his subjects, once more pointed at the body.

"To speak of the Gods is to disrespect the Aten, and to disrespect the Aten is to disrespect me. And to disrespect your pharaoh, your God among mortals is punishable by only one method."

Smiling, Kek turned towards the masses and shouted, "Death!"

The pharaoh then gave a dominant smirk. "Exactly."

As the masses all trembled before their tyrannical leader, Akhenaten simply waved at them.

"Now continue going about your business. It's a glorious day."

As Akhenaten turned back around and headed back into his palace, Kek and the Medjay began escorting the masses back to their villages. The pharaoh's lesson had concluded.

10
The Spark of Revolution
1340 B.C.

With everyone in the hall having finished their meal, they each began to form a queue so that they could wash their bowls. Chione was standing one space in front of Dakarai. He tapped her on the shoulder and leaned towards her.

"So how long have you been here?"

Chione turned around. "It's hard to keep track of the days now. I know it's been months, I just don't know how many." Dakarai nodded his head as Chione glanced down. "Not so far away from Amarna. My family and I sound very similar to yours. We lived in a small village. No more than about five other families were there. There were animals, every month Father would trek to the Nile to go fishing. He always preferred the taste of a fish that'd been in the Nile."

Chione teased a quick smile before a long tear began to roll down her cheek. She then glanced up at Dakarai. "But then they came. Kek. The Medjay. They destroyed my village, butchered my parents, and burnt my home to a crisp." Chione wiped her face as Dakarai placed his hand over her shoulder. She smiled at him.

"Akhenaten took everything I held close, and left me nothing, but pain and despair." Chione then embraced Dakarai. Surprised at her willingness to embrace him, he hugged her back. The two then shared a brief but intimate moment. For a few seconds at least, it appeared that they had finally found someone who could truly empathise with them on a personal level. As they both let go, Chione then looked into Dakarai's eyes.

"The pharaoh is all powerful, but you are right. He must be stopped." Chione then took Dakarai's hand. "Come with me. We must convince the others to stand with us." Chione then took Dakarai back into the living quarters. As they both looked around, they could see everyone sitting around, talking. At the back of the room, Chione spotted Abrax and Bast, who were playing a game of senet. She and Dakarai went over to sit with them. As they approached, Bast was looking confused.

"Erm, I think I'm going to have to move backwards."

Abrax looked rather puzzled at his friend's decision. "But Bast, there's a free square in front. You can go forward."

Bast's jaw lowered slightly, and his eyes began to squint. "Ah yes. I mean no. Ah. I must confess, Abrax, I have no idea what I'm doing."

Dakarai watched on as they continued to play. He was fascinated by their composure. "How do you both remain so calm given the current situation?"

Abrax turned to Dakarai. "Acceptance, my friend. Like Pilis told you, you're not the first to desire the pharaoh's blood, and you won't be the last. There was a point in time where Bast and I were the most optimistic of us all." He sighed. "But after seeing every attempt on the regime being crushed, Bast and I have just stopped believing now."

Chione shook her head, and Dakarai leaned forward. Acceptance was not an option for him. "This time, however, the plan changes. I'm not asking you to walk into certain death having achieved nothing but staining the royal palace with our blood. This time, we are going to send a statement. A statement that shoots straight through the heart of Egypt. We are going to show the pharaoh that now, his support dies."

Intrigued, both Abrax and Bast leant forward.

"What do you mean by that?"

Pumped up by his own words, Dakarai leant in even more. "I mean we don't march into Akhetaten, only to secure our destruction. We travel across the land, aiding every village that has been exterminated by the Medjay. We rally the survivors. We show them that hope is not lost. And when we've travelled the land, igniting the spirt and imagination of the people, then that is when we will strike."

Looking stunned, Abrax turned to Bast, and then back to Dakarai. "You mean…"

Dakarai nodded. "Yes. Once we have enough support and belief, we go to Akhetaten, and end this once and for all."

Slumping back in their seats, Abrax and Bast began to glance around once more, seemingly trying to conjure up an opposing argument. Neither one of them could think of one. Abrax, finally giving a smile, leant in towards Dakarai once more.

"Maybe I do have one final shred of hope left in me, or stupidity." Abrax then looked over at Bast. He smiled at his old friend. "What do you say, old friend? Care for one more adventure?"

Bast took Abrax's hand and squeezed it tight. He then gently nodded his head. Their hope had been reignited at last. The two friends then glanced back up at Dakarai and Chione. Abrax smiled.

"What's the plan?"

Chione then leant forward. "We need all the support we can get if we're going to carry out this quest. We need Pilis if we are to have a chance."

Dakarai took a deep breath.

"Let me talk to him. I know I didn't exactly make the best first impression, but I feel that he just needs some reminding of what hope feels like."

Standing up from his chair, Bast began to stretch. "And what shall we do?"

Dakarai and Chione both turned to each other in thought, before turning back towards Bast. "Now you two are to go around this refuge. You are to rally as much support for our cause as you can. You are to gather as much support in al-Minya as possible. We need everyone together if we are to stand a chance against the pharaoh."

As Abrax and Bast nodded their heads, Dakarai looked over at Chione. He took her hands. "Go with them. The more support we have, the better our odds. And besides, I feel I should speak to Pilis alone."

As Abrax and Bast headed off to find reinforcements, Chione then looked into Dakarai's eyes. The moment they shared was filled with intimacy. As the moment then passed, Chione kissed Dakarai on the head, and then ran off to catchup with Abrax and Bast. Looking over, now alone in the living quarters, Dakarai glanced over to see Pilis. He was also sitting alone, praying. As Dakarai took a deep breath, he headed over to the room where Pilis was praying. It was time for some persuasion.

11
Disturbance in Sanctuary
1340 B.C.

The refuge sanctuary was a small, darkened room with only one ray of light pouring down on Pilis. As Dakarai stood in the entrance to the sanctuary, Pilis had his back to him, as he continued to pray. He could however, sense Dakarai's presence.

"You know, this sanctuary is the one place where I can be myself. There are no Medjay or regime dictating my beliefs, and in here, I don't have to appear as the righteous leader that keeps this group safe. In here, I am but a child of the Gods."

Dakarai then slowly wandered inside the sanctuary, as Pilis turned around to face him.

"This is normally a place of privacy. Never more than one person in here at a time."

Dakarai took another deep breath. "Urgent matters require our attention. Our love for the Gods is irrelevant if we cannot practise our faith."

Pilis, sick and tired of Dakarai's stubbornness, sighed and turned away from him once more. "You still feed these people false hope. I've heard what you've been preaching to them. What did I tell you? We will not fight the invincible." Pilis began tidying up the sanctuary by picking up any small items that were littering its floor. Dakarai leant down to help him. Perhaps this would persuade him to help.

"Except he's not invincible. We possess one thing that he does not… hope. I've been here for one evening, and the hope that these people have is incredible. The desire for change is undeniable. And I don't believe for a second that you have completely given up yet."

As he finished tidying the floor, Dakarai then handed the last of the littered items to Pilis. He sighed. "Or maybe you have. Maybe you have given in. Then you're no better than the pharaoh himself."

Enraged by Dakarai's comment, Pilis slammed the tidied items onto one of the shelves at the back of the room. He then dropped his head in anger, although trying to remain composed in this sacred room.

Dakarai moved closer towards him. His tone was a lot calmer now. "We have a chance to right the wrongs of this regime. Together we can gather support from all across the empire. There will still be far more supporting our cause than those who will oppose it. We can finally bring an end to the chaos."

Unable to control his anger, Pilis turned to Dakarai and squared up to him. His fists were clenched. Dakarai though, stood his ground. "You know, when I first arrived here, I was a lot like you. I was convinced that I was going to be the one to end Akhenaten's slaughter. I saw myself as a hero. I saw myself joining the Gods up in the cosmos. But instead, do you know what I saw?"

Remaining silent, Dakarai did not even blink.

"I saw nothing but pain, and suffering. I saw Egyptian citizens handing each other to the Medjay in fear that they'd be taken themselves. I saw hundreds of men, women and children murdered in their homes. And for what? The paranoia and insanity of a disillusioned dictator. Our king, our supposed God was killing his own worshipers."

Trying to avoid further confrontation, Dakarai then stepped back as a tear fell down Pilis' cheek.

"That was when I learnt that this fight cannot be won. He's turned our own people against each other. He has the Medjay running around like dogs, killing innocent people for sport. This is when I learnt that the only thing to do is outrun it. Outrun the murders, outrun the betrayals, outrun everything. Run and hide, because if they catch you, you won't join the Gods. You'll be nothing but a pile of ash that no one remembers."

Having said his piece, Pilis then stormed out of the sanctuary, while Dakarai simply stood there motionlessly. As he watched Pilis storm away, Dakarai's head dropped, along with most of his optimism. With little else he could do, Dakarai made his way back into the living quarters.

As he wandered back into the living quarters, he heard the refuge entrance slam. Pilis must have left. Now alone inside the refuge, Dakarai sat down on one of the stalls and put his head in his hands. He sighed.

"Can this be true? Is there no cause to fight for anymore?" Brushing his hair back with his fingers, Dakarai sighed once more. "I'm not enough. What to do now?" As he looked around the room, struggling for what to think of next, Dakarai heard three knocks on the refuge entrance. Jumping to feet, Dakarai cautiously wandered over to the door. Standing on the other side, Dakarai was unsure of the secret code needed to enter the refuge. He took a deep breath.

"Hail to…"

He heard panting on the other side of the door. "Hail to the cause."

Tilting his head, this was a voice Dakarai recognised. "Chione, is that you?"

The panting was still heavy on the other side of the door. "Yes, let us in. We have good news."

As Dakarai opened the door, Chione, Abrax and Bast quickly ran inside. Bast was sweating and panting heavily; he despised manual labour. As they all ran inside and sat down, Dakarai closed the door behind them.

"Well? What is your news?"

As Chione was the first to get her breath back, she stepped forward, smiling. "Your words. Your plan. Your hope. Egyptians from all over al-Minya want to help."

To Chione's surprise, Dakarai simply shrugged his shoulders at her news. "I hope your quest was more profitable than mine. Pilis will take considerably more convincing to join our fight. How many people wanted to help us?"

Abrax then wiped the sweat from his forehead. He then too, stepped forward. "Follow us, Dakarai. Let us show you."

Clearly not as excited as the rest of them, Dakarai followed his new friends as they all headed for the refuge door. As they each left one by one, Dakarai laboriously followed on behind. He did not know it yet, but this was to be a pivotal day in his revolution.

12
Revolution is Born
1340 B.C.

Running through the al-Minya backstreets that were lit by nothing but the night sky, Chione, Abrax and Bast were desperate to show Dakarai their discovery. Dakarai though, was not sharing the same enthusiasm as his friends. As Chione glanced behind her, she noticed that Dakarai was beginning to fall behind. She called out to him. "Make haste, Dakarai. Don't get left behind."

As the rest of his friends turned a corner and disappeared from his sight, Dakarai was forced to speed up. Turning the corner down into another backstreet, he found Chione standing at the end of it. She simply glanced over and smiled at Dakarai. She was pointing to her right. "Down there. Come. Down there is how we win."

Unsure of what to expect, Dakarai cautiously made his way over to Chione. As he reached her, he turned to his left. Standing perfectly still, his eyes widened in amazement. With a tear rolling down his cheek, Dakarai knew that this was a sight of pure magnificence. Chione grasped Dakarai's hand and smiled once more.

"This is our hope. Pilis may struggle to see it now, but he will. In the meantime, what do you think the pharaoh will make of this?"

Dakarai looked out into the al-Minya bazaar to see hundreds of Egyptian citizens all facing him. As they all looked up, smiling, the children were playing and the elderly were clapping. Dakarai had not seen unity like this for a long, long time. Standing in front of the masses were Abrax and Bast. They too smiled at Dakarai. Abrax then raised his hand in the air.

"Hail to Neter."

In perfect unison, all of the citizens rose up and shouted together, "Hail to Neter". Then following Abrax's example, all rose their hands in the air. As Dakarai wiped the tears from his eyes, he turned to Chione, clearly very moved and starstruck.

"Thank you. Today the fight lives."

Chione then wrapped her arms around Dakarai and embraced him. Squeezing her tight, not only was Dakarai finding her a key ally involved in the revolution, but he was also falling for her. As they let go of each other, Dakarai then stepped out into the crowd of followers. They descended into a deafening silence as he approached them. They all stood in awe, as they waited for him to speak.

"Tonight, is a special night. Tonight, the revolution is born."

The crowd began to cheer as Dakarai raised his fist in the air. He was just as pumped up as the rest of them.

"The destruction caused by our Pharaoh has left the kingdom in tatters, and in desperate need of salvation. Well, when we have saved those survivors, whose families were butchered by the Medjay, we will storm Akhetaten and end Akhenaten's reign of terror once and for all."

The crowd continued to cheer, their volume increasing.

"No more will innocent people be slaughtered for practising their faith. No more will Egyptian citizens across the kingdom be persecuted for buying into the disillusioned madness that our pharaoh is so obsessed with."

As the cheers grew louder, even some of the older, weaker Egyptians couldn't help themselves but rise to their feet and join in the celebrations.

"This is a new era. The era of freedom."

As the cheering reached fever pitch, everyone was showing their passion and desire for revolution. Chione wrapped her arms around Dakarai. As Abrax and Bast joined in with the masses in cheering their new leader, Chione looked up at Dakarai.

"Is this the revolution you wanted?"

Dakarai then began to stroke Chione's hair. Looking down at her, he smiled. "No. This is better. We can finally put right all of the pain that we've felt. Now it is our time to strike back."

Chione smiled, herself. "So, what shall we do now?"

Glancing up at the moon, Dakarai was in thought. He gave a somewhat excitable grin.

"Get some rest. For tomorrow, we prepare."

13
The Perks of Power
1340 B.C.

It was morning in Akhetaten. The streets were filled with life. Families were wandering through the bazaar, looking for food to eat, and garments to wear. There were children playing all around the alleyways and around the streets. The infinite conversations could be heard all around the city. Merchants haggling with their customers, and the sounds of coins being dropped into various baskets and pockets could be heard every which way. However, this city buzzing with life soon became filled with nothing but terror. Wandering through the bazaar was Akhenaten. Aboard his sedan chair and being escorted by the Medjay, with General Kek leading from the front, the pharaoh was being escorted through the streets of his capital. With the citizens of Akhetaten all now frozen with fear, no one dared to make the next move with fear that it would be their last. As they made their way into the bazaar, Akhenaten looked down at one of the Medjay soldiers that was carrying his chair.

"Stop here. I want to take a walk."

The soldier nodded. "Yes, my Pharaoh."

As the soldiers placed the chair carefully down, one

of them jumped down onto all fours and moved to the side of the pharaoh's chair. Using the soldier almost like a stair, Akhenaten stepped onto his back, using it to help him climb down. As he stepped onto the ground, the pharaoh looked around at his surroundings, glaring at his subjects that had all moved well out of his way. He was in a dastardly mood, looking to exercise his power on whomever he could. Making his way over from the front of the convoy, Kek was confused as to why they had all stopped.

"What is it, my king? Why have we stopped?"

Akhenaten continued to look around. "What do you see, General?"

As Kek too, began looking around into the bazaar, he watched the citizens, all whom were now constantly looking over their shoulder with fear that they may be taken by the Medjay. Kek looked on at the uncomfortable masses and smiled.

"I see fear. I see obedience, and I see order."

Satisfied with his general's answer, the pharaoh too, gave a rather sinister grin.

"Exactly. The fear ensures the obedience, and obedience creates order. Never before has the empire been in the position that it is now. I have finally ensured peace and prosperity for my kingdom. I have finally fulfilled my destiny."

As Akhenaten basked in his glory, there were two children coming down one of the side streets, each playing with some small sticks. Not looking where they were going, they were headed straight for the pharaoh. Running at pace, one of the children bumped into the pharaoh, causing Akhenaten to jolt back, winded. As the young boy fell to the floor, he was instantly clawed upwards by General Kek, who raised him in the air.

"What are you doing? You dare touch your pharaoh? You dare suffer the consequences?"

With the child crying in mid-air, Kek pulled out the boy's left arm, with the intention of cutting it off. As the child begged for mercy, Kek's teeth were gritted. He got off on instances such as these. It was here, where his true power as leader of the Medjay could be demonstrated. With his blade raised in the air, the screams of the boy's father could be heard through the gathering of citizens that had assembled around the unfolding scene. The boy's father sprinting up to Kek, and dropped to his knees.

"Please, my Pharaoh, have mercy. He's just a boy. I beg you, please!"

After taking a moment to compose himself, Akhenaten made his way over, raising his hand in the air. "Calm yourself, General. It was an accident." Taking the blade from Kek, the pharaoh lowered the weapon, and patted the young boy on his head. Gesturing to Kek to put the boy down, he obliged. The child then began wiping the tears from his eyes. The pharaoh smiled. "It's okay. Children must be able to have fun, and what kind of pharaoh would I be if I punished this beautiful child?" Patting the child on the back, his smile began to look ever more genuine and sincere. "Go on. Run along."

Sprinting back to his father, the young boy jumped and embraced him, as if it were the last time he would ever see him. Kek turned to his king, glaring at him.

"My King, why?"

As he slowly began to lower his head, the pharaoh's smile began to look a lot more sinister. He then slowly turned his head towards the child's father, who was still embracing his son.

"Of course, someone does have to pay."

As Kek turned towards the pharaoh, his sinister grin matched that of Akhenaten. Pointing at the child's father, the elderly man turned around, terrified.

"I will never be embarrassed in front of my people. Your incompetence must be met with punishment. Seize him."

Lunging towards the child's father, two of the Mediay soldiers took him by the arms and began to drag him towards the pharaoh. With the man kicking and screaming, just like his son, he was begging to be set free.

"I'm sorry, my King. You are all powerful. Please spare me."

The pharaoh chuckled to himself. He glanced over at Kek, smiling. "You see, General? Fear causes obedience, and obedience results in order."

Kek nodded. Even he was impressed at the stranglehold his king possessed over the empire. "You are truly all powerful, my Pharaoh."

As the pharaoh held the long blade up in the air, the Medjay held out the man's arm, offering it to Akhenaten. As the man's son continued to cry and scream in terror, Akhenaten glared into the man's eyes, gritting his teeth.

"Never again will you forget that I am a God."

With the man still screaming, the pharaoh, with one swift stroke of his blade, swung down, cutting the man's arm clean off. As the man collapsed to the floor screaming in pain, blood was pouring everywhere. Two of the Medjay then picked him up and threw him back towards his son and the now dispersing crowd. Turning to Kek, the pharaoh's expression was one of total composure, despite the chaos.

"But out of all of those attributes, the most important is fear. Fear is what ensures my empire's prosperity." Turning back and stepping aboard his sedan chair, the pharaoh's lesson was over. It was time to move on. As the Medjay each took their positions around the chair, they all lifted it up. Akhenaten then pointed forwards into the distance.

"On we go. I wish to meet more of my loyal subjects."

As Kek made his way back over towards the front of the convoy, the rest of the Medjay began to move again. Crossing his arms, the pharaoh sat back in his chair, breathing in the morning air and basking in his dominance.

"And to think, one day I can pass on this legacy to my son." Akhenaten looked into the distance, grinning. "To an eternal dynasty."

As all of the Medjay carrying and guarding the pharaoh echoed his words, "To an eternal dynasty," they continued to make their way through the kingdom, for their king had more of his subjects to greet.

14
The First Triumph
1340 B.C.

It was morning in al-Minya, and as the sun continued its rise in the sky, there was an element of excitement in the air, for today was day one in the struggle for freedom. Leading his many followers, Dakarai had left the refuge and was taking his forces into the main square. Abrax and Bast were escorting the forces from the front, whereas Dakarai preferred to lead from behind. He and Chione were at the back of the convoy, constantly surveying what was in front of them. Chione turned to Dakarai.

"So what have you got planned for them?"

Dakarai continued to look on into the distance.

"We need to learn how to stand as one. Only then can we take the pharaoh's forces head on."

Chione tilted her head. "And how do you plan on testing that method?"

As the front of the convoy suddenly stopped, Abrax sprinted from the front, all the way back towards Dakarai and Chione. As he reached them, he pointed into the distance. "Dakarai, they are here. Should we get into position?"

Glancing at Chione, Dakarai smiled. "Yes. Move them quickly."

As Abrax nodded, he turned around and sprinted back up towards the front of the convoy. Chione meanwhile, turned to Dakarai. Her eyebrows were raised.

"What does he mean? Who is here?"

Dakarai took a deep breath.

"Late last night Abrax heard reports that Medjay troops were headed here, to keep us in line. Well not anymore. This is the first step on our quest for freedom. The Medjay must not take al-Minya."

As they arrived into the main square, Chione's jaw had dropped in surprise. Moving quicker, it was time to take up their positions all around the square. Hiding down backstreets and alleys, Dakarai led Chione to their position behind one of the market stools. Still completely stunned, she looked up at Dakarai.

"Has your mind turned against you? These people have no training, no weapons. How do you expect them to defeat the Medjay?"

Smirking at her, Dakarai began to survey the area. He was waiting for the Medjay.

"Like I said last night, all we need is hope, and the Gods will support us."

As the remainder of his forces each took up their positions around the square, Dakarai glanced over towards Abrax and Bast who were hiding on the far side of the square. Dakarai put his finger to his lips, as did

Abrax. They needed to stay quiet so to maintain the element of surprise. Leaning down next to Chione, Dakarai moved forward and whispered in her ear.

"Stay absolutely silent. When I give the signal, we move."

Confused, Chione shrugged her shoulders.

"What's the signal?"

Dakarai then winked at her, for everything was all planned out. "You'll know."

As Chione smiled, three Medjay soldiers had wandered into the square, all riding on horseback. To the right of the square, the soldiers noticed a lone elderly woman attending to her market stool. Grinning at the other two, one of the soldiers jumped off his horse and began making his way over to the lady. The other two soldiers remained atop their horses, following on just behind. Standing over the lady, the soldier glared at her.

"What do you think you are doing?"

Rather frail, the woman turned around to face the soldier, who towered over her. She was shaking. "I-I mean no harm, sir. I am simply trading from my stall."

The woman's stall was filled with fruit from different parts of the empire. Their colours lit up the stall with different shades and shapes. The soldier snatched an apple from the stall, and took a large bite out of it. The juice began dripping down his chin.

"And you conduct this business without permission from the royal guard?"

Dropping the apple to the ground, the soldier

booted a large hole in the side of the stall with his seemingly giant feet. With the stall unevenly supported, it collapsed to the ground, causing the fruit to spill out onto the ground and roll away. The woman's shaking intensified, despite her trying to remain perfectly still. Tears began streaming down her cheeks. Laughing at her fear, the other two soldiers watched on, completely amused at her expense. The soldier standing opposite her then removed a large sword from his belt. The fun and games were over.

"I take it you know the penalty for this kind of treachery?"

Unable to hide her tears, the woman glanced down at her left arm, where she modelled a long scar, owed to her last run in with the Medjay. The soldier smirked. Looking on at the injustice in front of them, Chione was beginning to get very agitated.

"We must move now. They are going to kill that woman. Where is your signal?

Nodding towards Abrax and Bast on the far side, it was time to put their plan into action.

Abrax and Bast began to lead their group into the square itself, towards the soldiers. Hearing what sounded like hundreds of footsteps headed towards them, the two Medjay on horseback turned around to inspect what was going on. Watching on, Dakarai then turned to Chione.

"Here we go."

Copying their forces on the far side, Dakarai,

Chione and the rest of their forces began to slowly wander towards the Medjay. The solider standing over the woman, clutching his sword finally began to hear the disruption, so just like his men, turned around to investigate. As his jaw dropped, sweat began trickling down his forehead. Stepping away from the elderly woman, the Medjay could not believe what they were seeing. Tensing every muscle in his body, the soldier looked around at Dakarai's growing forces, now beginning to surround him and his men. The soldier stood his ground, though his left eye began to twitch.

"How dare you all intrude on Medjay business. Disperse immediately, or suffer the consequences."

Completely ignoring him, Dakarai and his forces continued to walk towards them. Taking this moment to escape the impending chaos, the elderly woman ran over and hid behind what was left of her collapsed market stall. Completely surrounded, the Medjay on horseback began to slowly move backwards. In a mad rage, the soldier clutching his sword began waving it around in an attempt to intimidate Dakarai and his followers. It did not work. Surrounded by hundreds of Egyptian citizens, the three Medjay were now trapped.

"Was I not clear? Leave or you will die. All of you."

Raising his arm in the air, Dakarai stopped in the middle of the square, as did his forces. They all stood no more than ten metres away from the Medjay. Glaring into the eyes of the soldier clutching his sword, Dakarai stepped forward, alone.

"You have no business here. It is you that needs to leave."

Insulted, the soldier's bloodshot eyes widened. Pointing his sword directly at Dakarai, he began to move forward. Though still failing to be intimidated, Dakarai continued to walk towards him. As the two men then stopped just a metre apart from one another, the soldier's pointed sword was just able to brush Dakarai's nose. He glared at the young man.

"What did you say, boy? You dare defy the orders of a Medjay soldier? Do you have any idea what we are going to do to you?"

As the two Medjay on horseback glanced at each other, it was clear that their concern was growing. Pushing the sword away from his face, Dakarai began to tense up, gritting his teeth.

"Let me tell you what is going to happen. You will leave al-Minya, and you will never return. You will journey back to Akhetaten and tell your Pharaoh that his days are numbered. His reckoning is coming."

In contrast to the soldiers on horseback who began to look terrified, the soldier in front of Dakarai began to chuckle as he digested the younger man's threat. He was still clutching his sword tightly.

"You truly believe that you and these rats could storm the holy city? You are clearly very foolish."

Smirking at the soldier, as Dakarai opened his mouth once more so to speak, he began to hear a very familiar voice coming through the crowd of his followers.

"We may not be able to stop the madness at Akhetaten. But I can make one promise… we are more than capable of stopping you right now."

As Dakarai glanced behind him, he watched in amazement as an old face made his way through the crowd, walking towards him. It was now clear that his revolution was ready. Pilis had joined the fight. Standing at the front of the forces next to him, Pilis led with Dakarai as his followers continued to once more walk towards the Medjay. Now clenching his sword with all his might, the soldier lunged forward and swung his sword towards Dakarai. Before the blade had chance to connect with Dakarai's face, Bast lunged forward and grabbed the soldier's hand. Squeezing it until the soldier dropped his sword, Bast then continued to squeeze even harder, until he could hear the bones in the soldier's hand crack. As Bast let go, the soldier dropped to his knees, screaming in pain. Using his other arm, he laboriously clambered back aboard his horse. Unwilling to stay and fight, the three Medjay turned their horses around and began to ride away from al-Minya. Looking back towards Dakarai, the soldier had tears running down his face. He was in extreme pain, but experiencing even greater embarrassment.

"You will not get away with this. You will all die."

As the Medjay rode off into the distance, everyone in the square began to cheer and embrace one another.

Even the elderly lady came out from her hiding place to join in the celebrations. With the excitement and joy clearly sketched onto everyone's face, Pilis wandered over to Dakarai. He patted his shoulder.

"Thank you, Dakarai. I'm sorry for before. You have given me a gift that I thought was gone forever. You have given me hope."

As the two men shared a long overdue embrace, Chione approached them. She too wrapped her arms around Dakarai.

"You were right. The revolution does live. Do you really think those soldiers will tell the pharaoh what happened here?"

Dakarai nodded his head. "I do."

Chione leaned forward. "So what shall we do now?"

Dakarai looked out into the distance. He sighed. "We must continue across Egypt. Giving hope back to the people. Once that is done, and only when that is done, we can head to Akhetaten and end the pharaoh's reign once and for all."

Both Chione and Pilis nodded in agreement. Pilis then looked out into the distance. "So where shall we liberate next?"

Following Pilis' gaze, Dakarai pointed out into the distance. "I believe there's a Medjay stronghold in the centre of Sohag."

With a determined look on his face, Pilis gestured that they get moving. He was pumped up now. "Then to

Sohag we will go."

Glancing around at his followers, still dancing, hugging, and celebrating victory, Dakarai smiled. He knew that difficult times were on the horizon, but for this small window of time, he felt nothing but comfort and pride. Looking up to the heavens, a tear began rolling down his cheek as he blew a kiss up to his parents. The fight for freedom had begun.

15
A Royal Retaliation
1340 B.C.

Sitting on his throne in the palace hall, Akhenaten was
entertaining his family. As his gorgeous bride Nefertiti
cradled in her arms the infant that would be king,
Tutankhamen, the pharaoh was desperately trying to
maintain an essence of family life in these violent and
treacherous times. As their servants continued to feed
them grapes and pour drinks into their chalices, what
was a moment of peaceful tranquillity soon turned into
testosterone fuelled rage. Storming into the hall,
General Kek had brought in with him three soldiers, the
soldiers who had been forced out of al-Minya by
Dakarai and his forces. As Kek approached the royal
family, he stopped and bowed his head. The other
soldiers copied.

"My apologies for disturbing you at this hour, my
King."

Almost leaping to his feet, the pharaoh was not
expecting an intrusion such as this. "What is the
meaning of this, General?"

Turning to the soldiers behind him, Kek glared at
the three of them intently. "These men have been run

out of al- Minya. They claim a revolution has begun, against your will, my King. They say a rebellion plans to rid the empire of all the Medjay, and of you."

With a seemingly shocked look on his face, the pharaoh slowly began to walk over to the three soldiers. "Is this true? Did they harm you?"

The soldier in the middle of the three, clutching his broken hand, nodded his head. "It is true, my Pharaoh. One of them broke my hand."

With a very uncharacteristic look of sympathy the pharaoh glanced down at the soldier's broken hand. "My dear boy. Let me see."

As the solider offered his hand out towards the pharaoh, Akhenaten began to inspect it. After a few moments, he then glanced up and glared into the soldier's eyes. Clutching the broken hand, the pharaoh began to squeeze it harder and harder. As more of the bones began to crack, the soldier dropped to his knees, screaming in pain. Then, as he suddenly chose to let go of the soldier's hand, Akhenaten made his way back over to his throne. Shielding their infant's eyes from the senseless violence in front of them, Nefertiti had no intention of introducing their son to this world yet. Simply shaking his head, Akhenaten was as calm as he was furious.

"No, my dear. Let him see. If he is to rule the empire one day, let him see how we punish cowards and traitors."

Resentfully, Nefertiti slowly pulled her hands away

from Tutankhamen's eyes. Terrified that her son could now see the brutality that his father was capable of, she was shaking. She glanced over at Akhenaten, seemingly trying to avoid eye contact with the soldiers. "What are you going to do, my King?"

With the most sinister of grins trying to fill his face, the pharaoh nodded at General Kek. "Teach them the price of failure."

Removing his sword from its belt, with one devastatingly swift motion, Kek steered his blade through the stomach of the middle soldier. As his now motionless body dropped to the floor like a rag doll, the other two Medjay shot around and attempted to flee the pharaoh's palace. Though before they could even reach the hall's exit, their path was cut off by other members of the royal guard. Beginning to move forward, these soldiers then began slowly pushing the two treacherous soldiers back towards the pharaoh. As Kek cleaned the blood from his sword, the two remaining soldiers fell to their knees before him and the pharaoh. They were both sobbing uncontrollably.

"Please, my Pharaoh, have mercy. We will never fail you again."

Staring almost straight through the eyes of the soldiers, the pharaoh's stare was now almost catatonic. "Correct. You will never fail me again."

Without any more warning, Kek once more raised his blade in the air, and with two more lightening strokes, killed the other two soldiers. As their bloody corpses began staining the palace floor, Kek turned towards Akhenaten.

"What does this mean, my King?"

Turning towards the general, Akhenaten was clearly looking uneasy. "A rebellion, they said? They must be silenced before the people of Akhetaten can hear about it. I want you to take the best Medjay soldiers we have, and I want you to find them. If you have to journey across the entirety of the empire, I want you to find them, and exterminate them."

With his fists clenched and his teeth grit, Kek knew just the soldiers to aid him on his quest. "My pleasure, my King. Very soon no one will know they even existed."

The pharaoh then pointed towards the hall exit. "Now go. We must make haste. Return when they are all dead."

Kek then bowed before the pharaoh. "As you wish, my King."

As Kek then turned around and left the hall, Akhenaten gingerly wandered back over towards his wife and son. As he almost collapsed on his throne, Nefertiti turned to him. "Do you think that Kek will truly be able to dispose of this rebellion?"

Akhenaten glanced at his wife, and then slowly made his way over to his young son. Picking up the heir to his throne, the pharaoh looked down into his eyes, and kissed the baby on the forehead. He smiled. "He will be ruthless. This massacre will be no different to that of those treacherous preachers that once infested my empire."

Looking rather concerned, Nefertiti took a deep breath. "You're sure?"

Turning to his wife, in what seemed like an instant, the pharaoh's look of worry had transformed into a stare of pure viciousness. "That I am."

16
Elite Reinforcements
1340 B.C.

The royal armoury was a place filled with testosterone and passion. The Medjay lived and died for their pharaoh, and would smite down anyone whom would dare stand in his way. Wandering into the armoury, this was the perfect place to recruit more soldiers, though ordinary soldiers were not what Kek was after. Storming past the lower ranking Medjay, they all stood up straight to attention as their general wandered past them. However, these soldiers were not good enough. Storming down a long, narrow corridor, Kek arrived at a much darker, colder section of the armoury. There was no noise or natural light, just candles scattered around the floor. Sitting in front of Kek in a circle sat five hooded men, the Medjay Elites. The most heavily trained and feared group of soldiers in the entire empire. Realising Kek's presence, one of the hooded men turned around. His hood was still covering his face.

"General Kek. To what do we owe this privilege?"

Kek took a deep breath before responding. "Your skills are required again. There is a rebellion against the pharaoh."

Another of the Elites then turned around and faced the general. "And I take it you want us to make it disappear?"

Kek nodded his head. "You are to accompany me, all of you. We are to find that group of scarabs and crush them once and for all."

A third Medjay Elite then turned around. All of their faces were still totally covered by their hoods. "Are you sure the empire is ready for our reign of destruction to return?"

Smirking, Kek's mind turned back to the last time the Elites were called into action, and the devastation they caused. "Your methods are effective, and at this time, utterly essential."

As all five of the Medjay Elites began to stand up, they each removed their hoods. All being bald, their faces and bodies were covered in tattoos of the ancient spirit of evil, Apep; a good luck charm for such a violent group of soldiers. As they each took their blades and placed them in their scabbards, they all turned to General Kek. One of the Elites stepped forward, wearing a sinister grin.

"Come, General. Let us find these scarabs."

17
Continued Liberation
1340 B.C.

Standing at the edge of the Sohag village, a group of ten Medjay soldiers were staring down Dakarai and his growing following. Armed with swords and on horseback, the soldiers were waiting for the rebellion to take their first steps in this stalemate. Looking on at the soldiers in front of him, Dakarai smiled. Abrax turned to Dakarai. He was not sharing the same amusement.

"They knew we were coming?"

Dakarai glanced over at Abrax. "They are terrified of us. And they should be."

Clutching Dakarai's hand, Chione looked up at him. She shared his optimism. "What shall we do?"

Looking back over at the soldiers protecting the village entrance, and then glancing back down at Chione, Dakarai smiled once more. "We do what we came here to do. We liberate."

Standing firm by the village entrance, the Medjay captain stepped forward, raising his sword in the air. "Stand firm. No mercy. No prisoners."

All of the soldiers around him then blasted at the top of their lungs, "Hail to the Pharaoh," before stepping forward.

Dakarai and his forces then did the same. As Dakarai raised his arm in the air, a sea of his forces bellowed out, "Hail to Neter."

Sprinting towards each other, it was time for the next battle to commence.

As the sun began to set in the Sohag main square, the group of Medjay now either scattered the ground, dead, or were retreating into the desert. Standing as one, Dakarai and his forces stood tall in the village. As the locals began gathering around them, they each began cheering, and wandering around offering food and drink. As they continued to celebrate another victory, Dakarai, with Chione and Pilis standing next to him, looked around at all of the Egyptian citizens filling the square. They were all approaching him, for he was their hero, their saviour. Looking around at all of them, Dakarai took a deep breath.

"Sohag is saved. But the fight continues. We are a strong force, but we will be even stronger if you join our cause. Help us restore freedom to the land once more."

With the crowd continuing to cheer, Pilis then stepped forward, standing next to Dakarai. "We will liberate the empire, and then love for the Gods will return."

With the crowd cheering, Dakarai pointed towards the seemingly endless desert. "Then let us move. We will head to Akhetaten, freeing every village we come across along the way. Onwards. Freedom awaits."

As Dakarai then began to make his way towards Akhetaten, his now increasing forces began to follow on behind. He knew that it would not be easy, and he knew that at some point they would run into more Medjay and resistance. But that did not bother him. It was time to storm the capital.

18
Hunted on the Nile
1340 B.C.

After weeks of travelling, Dakarai and his forces were beginning to tire. As the elderly began to faint, children were crying out for some water to drink. Wandering up to the front of the convoy, Abrax wanted to share his concerns.

"Dakarai, we need to rest. The people will not make it to Akhetaten if we keep moving for much longer."

Looking back at his shattered forces, Dakarai knew that it would not be long before their exhaustion took its toll. Turning to Abrax, he nodded. "Yes. We will rest. We must make sure everyone gets some water. Then we will get moving again."

Heeding Dakarai's orders, Abrax and Bast began escorting groups of people down to the river. Those who could swim simply leapt in and began washing themselves in the glistening water that the sun was reflecting off. Turning to Dakarai, Pilis then decided to wander down the far side of the river.

"I'm just going to scout the perimeter. Just to make sure we are safe."

Walking up to Dakarai, Chione took his hand. She

looked up at him and smiled. "They needed this. We must ensure they stay healthy. We've been travelling for days, and Akhetaten will be like nothing we've ever encountered before."

Dakarai nodded. For the first time in their quest, it appeared that everyone could enjoy a brief moment of tranquillity, far away from the bloodshed they were now so used to. Although this moment of peace, as delicate as it was, neared its devastating end. Looking out into the distance, Dakarai began to hear shouting. As he glanced down the Nile, he and Chione could just about make out Pilis, sprinting towards them. His screams were getting louder.

"Run. Get moving. They're coming."

Looking past Pilis, both Dakarai and Chione could only watch in horror as a group of six Medjay galloped towards them. With a spine-tingling grin, Kek could finally home in on his target, for he and his Elites had found the rebellion. Speeding up as they crossed into an attack formation, Kek glanced over at Dakarai. Slowing his horse down, the general couldn't help but feel a strange feeling of déjà vu.

"The boy from the Waset river. Impossible."

As the Medjay Elites then began to split into two teams, they each galloped down either side of Dakarai's forces, trapping them. Now totally vulnerable to attack, Dakarai's forces had no escape. Surrounding the masses, the Elites suddenly stopped, in order to await Kek's instruction. As he jumped off of his horse, Kek began slowly walking towards Dakarai and his followers. Despite Abrax and Bast trying to retain an element of composure amongst their ranks, there was nothing but sheer terror floating through the followers. As he stopped directly in front of Dakarai, Kek stood no more than five metres away from the young man. He looked into Dakarai's eyes and smiled.

"I thought you were dead. No matter, we can rectify that now."

Clenching his fists, Dakarai too, stepped forward. "You will not stop us. Your reign of terror has come to an end. Peace will return to this land."

As Kek began to chuckle at his rival's confidence, he raised his arm in the air, causing all five of the Elites to dismount from their horses. They each took out their blades, waiting for the order to attack.

"You impress me, boy. You are strong and determined. Your mother on the other hand, she screamed like a whore as I sliced her throat."

Having heard enough, Dakarai began sprinting towards Kek. It was time to pay for that comment. Waiting for Dakarai to reach him, Kek clenched his raised fist, causing the Elites to begin their attack. Sprinting towards Dakarai's forces, they remained in perfect formation, ensuring Dakarai's forces were still trapped. As Dakarai neared his intended target, Kek tried to pull his sword out from its scabbard, but it was stuck. Before he was able to remove it, Dakarai leapt forward and tackled him to the ground. With a clean left hook, he punched Kek across the face. It did little damage. Years of fighting had left the general with a very high tolerance for pain. Dakarai's punch did little more than anger him further. Thrusting his head forward, Kek head-butted Dakarai with such force, it caused the boy to fall to his knees. Standing to his feet, Kek then spat out some blood onto the ground, seemingly marking his territory. Finally removing his sword, he raised it in the air as he looked down at Dakarai.

"You will be the last to go. You will first witness your rebellion die."

Sprinting towards the chaos unfolding in front of him, Kek wanted Dakarai to see the punishment he was going to administer. As Dakarai was able to gather himself and regain his awareness, he could only stare in horror at the massacre taking place in front of him. Kek and his Elites were cutting down everything in their path. Their situation was now desperate. Dakarai's followers were being taken out one by one. On the near side of the conflict, Abrax and Bast were standing back-to-back as they continued to fend off any Elite that tried to challenge them. In the centre of the battle, Chione and Pilis were huddled around the children and elderly. Dakarai had to get back involved, as his forces were dwindling fast. As he ran back towards the fight as fast as his legs could carry him, he found a sword on the ground that would have been dropped by one of his followers. Picking it up, he spotted one of the Elites about to sneak up on Chione from behind. Running up behind him, Dakarai raised the sword in the air.

"No."

With one swift thrust, Dakarai steered the sword through the Elite's back, causing him to scream and then collapse to the floor, dead. He then grabbed Chione's hand and turned her around to face him. He kissed her. "Stay close. No one else is going to die today."

Having taken Chione's hand, both Dakarai and Chione continued to fend off the seemingly relentless attacks that the Elites were mustering. Engrossed in the carnage all around her, Chione looked around, in search of a friend.

"Dakarai, where's Pilis?"

Dakarai paused for a brief moment in order to look around the battlefield, hoping to see his friend. To his left he spotted Pilis fighting off two of the Medjay Elites himself. To his amazement, Pilis was holding his own, but as their fight raged on, Dakarai could only watch in horror as an all too familiar foe began to sneak up on Pilis from behind. Raising his blade in the air, General Kek steered it straight through Pilis' shoulder blades. As the immense impact pushed Pilis forward, he then began laboriously coughing up blood, before collapsing to the floor. Dakarai's jaw dropped.

"Pilis. No."

With Pilis laying almost motionless on the ground, Kek spat on him. All he saw was another traitor to the empire. Looking round the battlefield, Dakarai's forces had been cut down by nearly half, although, the intensity of the fight was taking its toll on Kek's Elites, who were beginning to tire. Raising his arm in the air, he was convinced their mission was complete.

"Come now. Our job is complete. Let us return to Akhetaten. Let the rebellion die in the sun."

As the remaining Elites began their retreat over towards the general, Kek looked over at Dakarai, almost staring straight through him.

"Mourn your dead, boy. For this is mercy. You have nothing left. The sun will blister your skin, and then the vultures will pick at your corpse. Today, the rebellion is dead." Jumping back on their horses, Kek and the rest of the Medjay Elites began to ride off into the desert. Part of the Nile had turned red on account of all the blood that now filled it. Injured, but lucky to be alive, Abrax and Bast were attempting to aid the injured. Bast was helping a young woman to her feet.

"That's it. Slowly. You should be okay." Glancing at Abrax, Bast continued wiping sweat from his forehead.

"Abrax, where is Pilis?"

Standing almost catatonic, with a tear running down his face, Abrax could not take his eyes off Dakarai and Chione as they stood over the body of their swiftly dying friend. Dropping to his knees, Dakarai took Pilis' hand and clutched it tight. As Pilis struggled to take his final breaths, Dakarai then also held his head up in an attempt to make his final moments more comfortable.

Looking up at Dakarai, Pilis' eyes began to grow heavy.

"I'm sorry, Dakarai."

Tears were streaming down Dakarai's face. "For what? You have nothing to be sorry for."

With the last moments that he could muster, Pilis teased a smile. "You brought hope back into my life, Dakarai. For that I am eternally grateful." As Dakarai's grip on his friend's hand tightened, Pilis' began to loosen. "These people. Their sheer determination and will is enough to win this fight. T-take them to Akhetaten. Stop the pharaoh, and restore peace to the land. I will help you as much as I can in the next life."

Kneeling down next to Dakarai, Chione kissed Pilis on the forehead. By now Dakarai's grip was at its tightest.

"No. Fight harder. You are not going like this." As Pilis began to slowly loosen his grip on Dakarai's hand, it slowly dropped to the ground, and Pilis' eyes began to close.

"Hail to Neter."

As Pilis took his final breath, his eyes closed fully. For now, he was free. With tears streaming down everyone's face, Dakarai wiped his eyes and stood up. Looking around at the bodies that scattered the ground, and glancing up at the survivors, he needed to rally his troops more than ever now. He stepped forward.

"The deaths that we have suffered here today will not be in vain. Pilis, and everyone that has fought alongside us, dead or alive, deserves to see our struggles end in success. We will journey on. We will reach Akhetaten, and we will end the regime."

Cautious of Dakarai's words, Abrax stepped forward. "But Dakarai, half of us are dead. What chance do we stand against the pharaoh now?"

Wiping one last tear from his eye, Dakarai glanced up at the sky. "We have will, we have hope, and with some spirits I know who are watching over us in the next life, we have every chance."

Walking up towards Dakarai, Chione wrapped her arms around him, and then she too faced their remaining followers. "He's right. We must continue our quest. We cannot let these people, our friends, die in vain."

Some of the remaining survivors began to nod their heads in support, and quietly began cheering, almost under their breaths. Abrax turned to his old friend, Bast, and the two of them shared a warm embrace. Abrax then turned to face Dakarai and Chione.

"You're right. Let's journey on. Hail to Neter."

Bast joined his friend in voicing his support. "Hail to Neter."

Everyone then bowed to Dakarai before all shouting in seemingly perfect unison, "Hail to Dakarai. Hail to Neter."

Still with her arms wrapped around him, Chione looked up at Dakarai. "You're a hero to them. You're more of a God than Akhenaten will ever be."

Smiling at Chione, Dakarai then stepped out towards his passionate followers. He raised his arm in the air.

"We will move. It's time we sent shockwaves throughout the empire. Let us continue to Akhetaten." As Dakarai glanced up at the sky once more, it did not matter whether they were injured or not, every one of his surviving followers were up in arms, cheering for their leader. They were all in awe of him. Dakarai had restored a hope that many had thought was lost forever. Now, even in this time of need, his followers were still prepared to stand by his side. The time had come. It was time to venture to the capital. Akhetaten awaited.

19
Contrasting Opinions
1340 B.C.

As Kek and the remaining Mediay Elites stormed into the royal chambers, Akhenaten leapt to his feet. With his warriors returning from battle, the pharaoh needed to hear of their success. With blood and sweat dripping down from the soldier's heads, tired yet victorious, they bowed and knelt down before their king. The pharaoh stepped forward.

"General, you have returned. Tell me, did they suffer?"

Wiping the sweat from his forehead, Kek stood to his feet. "The rebellion is over, my King. Their forces are now minuscule. They stand no chance against you."

As the pharaoh began to make his way back towards his throne, he paused for a moment. After a brief intermission of silence, the pharaoh slowly glanced up at Kek. His eyes were wide open.

"Minuscule? But you exterminated them all. Didn't you?"

Kek sighed. "The fight was long, and there were more of them than I initially expected. We took a loss ourselves, but their forces were decimated. The handful that lives, will bury their dead and then most likely die of exhaustion themselves. The rebellion has been silenced."

Enraged, Akhenaten stormed over towards his general and squared up to him. Kek stood his ground, with the two of them looking as if they were going to collide at any minute. Kek was the taller man, but only just. He began gritting his teeth as the pharaoh continued to push his forehead up against his own. Furious, the pharaoh's bloodshot eyes met the gaze of Kek's.

"I gave you one task; to wipe out those who defy me, and you cannot do it. You say those who are left will die of exhaustion, but you do not know that. Who knows what they could be doing? Recruiting, building up another army? The empire is not safe until they are all dead."

The pharaoh then turned away from Kek. Now it was the general who was moving towards him. "If they place a single foot in Akhetaten, I will slaughter them myself."

The pharaoh turned back towards Kek. "I hope so, General. For your own sake."

Irate, both Kek and the pharaoh simply glared at one another. Their prosperous relationship was now reaching its boiling point. As they continued to stare each other down, Kek then simply turned around and began to make his way out of the chambers. The Elites too, followed on behind. One of them glanced back towards the pharaoh on his way out.

"Have a pleasant evening, noble one."

As Kek and the Elites left the pharaoh's chambers, he wandered over to his balcony. Staring out over his empire as the sun continued to rise, for the first time in his life, Akhenaten felt threatened. He glanced up towards the sky, and sighed.

"I assure you. This dynasty will be eternal. Nothing will stand in my way. I will remain a God, Father."

20
The Longing Touch of Passion
1340 B.C.

With the least injured of Dakarai's forces supporting those who were most injured, everyone was working together to ensure they were able to reach Akhetaten in time. On the edge of the Nile stood the remains of a small village, one that looked as though it met its demise at the hands of the Medjay long ago. Nevertheless, it would more than suffice as a place of shelter for Dakarai and his forces. Abrax and Bast were helping the older, more seriously hurt Egyptians onto whatever soft materials they could find. In these dark, ancient times, comfort was very much a privilege. Dakarai and Chione were helping the children. In the centre of the village, Dakarai found the remains of a small shack. With a collection of different animal hides inside, it was the perfect place to ensure the children stayed warm overnight. Inside the shack, Dakarai took the hides and spread them all out onto the floor, under the stars. Looking over at the children, he called them over.

"Here now, young ones. You can sleep here tonight."

As the children ran over and began fighting over

who got to sleep with the biggest hide, walking slowly, behind the other children was a young girl. She was both the youngest and smallest of the children. Walking over to Dakarai, she simply wrapped her arms around his waist, and hugged him tight. Dakarai hugged her back. He then knelt down so he could look her in the eye.

"Soon it will all be okay. Go on now. Get some sleep."

As the young girl then ran along to join the other children, Dakarai stood up. As Chione walked up to him, she too, wrapped her arms around him. She then glanced over at the children.

"All the blood. All the chaos, and yet it does not bother them at all."

Dakarai then kissed her on the forehead. "They are fearless. And that is what we will have to be where we're going."

As everyone appeared settled down for the night, Abrax and Bast wandered over towards Dakarai.

"Everyone is comfortable. Well, as comfortable as possible."

Patting both Abrax and Bast on the shoulder, Dakarai smiled. "Thank you. Get some rest yourselves. Tomorrow is the biggest day in our history."

Both Abrax and Bast then hugged Chione goodnight and nodded their heads towards Dakarai. Bast leant forward.

"You do think we are going to win, don't you Dakarai?"

Dakarai sighed. "We have to. Because if we do not, then we have no chance. Belief will win us this fight."

Bast teased a smile before he and Abrax went over to join the others in getting some much-needed sleep. Dakarai then took Chione's hand.

"Come, it is time we got some rest too."

He took Chione over to one of the abandoned shacks. It was almost reduced to rubble, but somehow still standing. There were more animal hides on the inside. As Dakarai took them, he arranged them on the floor so that he and Chione would at least have some comfort as they rested for the night. As they both laid down on the hides, they put their arms around each other and shared a warm embrace. Dakarai then kissed her forehead. Chione then looked up at him.

"What you said to Bast, do you truly believe it? Do you truly believe that after today we will win?"

Dakarai sighed once more before taking a deep breath. So engrossed with what Dakarai was about to say was she, Chione did not even blink.

"Like I said, I have to. It's belief that stopped the Medjay from killing everyone today, and it's the belief that will carry these people on to Akhetaten and dethrone the regime. If uncertainty begins to fill the minds of our followers, then it will consume them, and freedom will once again only be an impossible dream."

Chione continued to hug Dakarai tighter. "Are you scared?"

Looking deep into Chione's eyes, Dakarai was now

the one refusing to blink. The conviction on his face was clear. "I'm completely terrified. But I'm more terrified of this land living in fear for future generations, and that is what will drive me on."

Chione then pressed her head against Dakarai's chest, and closed her eyes. For the first time in many years, she was comfortable and, even if only for this brief night, relaxed.

"You know, Pilis was right. You did restore his hope. You restored hope for all of us. You have done something that no one else has ever dreamed of. You're taking on the pharaoh's regime, and you're proving to him that we are not going anywhere until freedom is restored; until all Gods are once more a part of our culture. I've never met anyone like you in my entire life. I love you."

Dakarai glanced down at Chione and smiled. He then pulled her in close. "I love you."

The two of them began to kiss. There was a great, primal passion in the air as the two of them began to indulge in each other's bodies. As they continued to kiss, Dakarai pulled one of the animal hides over the top of them, covering them both. Neither of them had ever felt emotions like these before; love, passion, lust. It was time for their true feelings for one another to be revealed.

21
The Day of Destiny
1340 B.C.

It was time. One of the most pivotal moments in their history was about to take place. Dakarai, holding Chione's hand, and with Abrax and Bast standing by his side, was looking out at his remaining followers. Well rested and ready to play their part, everyone was ready. The last of those who were washing themselves in the Nile were all climbing out to join the others who were standing with Dakarai. Looking out at his followers with a great sense of pride, Dakarai stepped forward.

"Today. Today is the most important day of our lives. The events that take place today will be celebrated by generations a thousand years from now. Today, we reunite the Gods with their people." Dakarai then pointed into the distance. "Over there is the city of Akhetaten. That is our destination. I know that some of you are carrying serious injuries from our last run in with the regime. Don't think of them as injures. Think of them as trophies. They are proof that the regime tried to take you down, and they are proof that they failed in doing so. Your heart and determination have brought us this far. So why can't they take us all the way."

His followers began nodding their heads in agreement.

Dakarai then took a deep breath. "I don't know what is going to happen when we get there, or what greeting our noble pharaoh has waiting for us. But I can tell you that whatever we are faced with, we will face it together. For this is the day that will be immortalised in our history. For today, freedom is restored. Hail to Neter."

Altogether, Dakarai's followers shouted "Hail to Neter," in near perfect unison. Glancing down at Chione, he kissed her. Then looking back up into the distance towards Akhetaten, Dakarai simply said one word, "Onwards."

As they made their way through the final leg of their quest, Dakarai knew that the time had come. Revenge was near. For this was his destiny.

22
The One-Man Mutiny
1340 B.C.

Sat in the royal hall with his wife, Nefertiti, next to him, the pharaoh was seeking council with the high priest. As their discussions continued, a lone Medjay soldier stormed into the hall. Running this way had caused his breathing to be heavy. Almost jumping out of his throne in anger, Akhenaten glared at the solider.

"What is the meaning of this?"

The soldier continued to fight his fatigue as he tried to get his breath back and compose himself. "Out in the desert. S-some of the soldiers saw a group of Egyptian citizens marching here. I think it's the rebellion."

As his eyes at first widened, the pharaoh's expression seemingly morphed into a sinister grin. This was the moment he had been waiting for. He began to chuckle.

"Alert General Kek. I want him and the rest of the Elites at the entrance to the city, and I want another team of Medjay guarding my chambers. They will not reach me."

The soldier nodded his head. "Of course, my King."

As the soldier then ran out of the hall in order to

alert the general, Nefertiti turned to her king.

"What is happening? Are we safe here?"

Akhenaten continued to smile. He was ready. "Just the reminder of a rebellion that will soon be crushed. Go and check on my son. By the time you return all will be as it was."

Nefertiti then stood up and left the royal chambers so to check on the young prince, Tutankhamen. Wandering over to his balcony, he took one final look out at the kingdom he'd spent years beating into submission. He smiled once more.

"It is time for General Kek to redeem himself."

Back down in the royal armoury, the lone Medjay was furiously searching for General Kek. Eventually finding him sitting on the far side of the armoury, the soldier cautiously wandered over to him. The general was sat leaning forward, the picture of composure. The soldier took a deep breath.

"General, the pharaoh has requested you. The rebellion; they're coming. He wants you and the Elites to guard the entrance to the city."

Kek chuckled at the sound of his pharaoh's name. He began sharpening his blade as he looked over at the soldier.

"Tell the pharaoh that the rebellion will be exterminated. And tell him, once order has been restored, I will be making some changes to this empire. Now go."

As the soldier ran out of the armoury, Kek

continued sharpening his blade. Once he had finished, he stood up, and slowly began to make his way towards the city entrance, with an ever more sinister grin as he did.

"Considerable changes indeed."

23
A Battle for the Ages
1340 B.C.

No more than one-hundred metres from the city entrance, Dakarai and his followers stood ready to lay siege on the capital. Tired from their travels, but ready to fight, they all stood and waited for the order to attack. Armed with weapons that they had found in the abandoned village, this time they were ready to go to war. This time they had their equalisers. Dakarai, with Chione, Abrax and Bast by his side, was staring almost catatonically at the city entrance. It appeared to be empty, with no one guarding it. Bast then turned to Dakarai.

"No one's here to greet us. This could be simpler than we thought."

Dakarai continued looking out at the entrance. "They are out there. They are waiting for us. We must tread with caution. Follow me. We move now."

Dakarai and his forces then slowly moved towards the entrance. As they got around twenty metres outside, seemingly out of nowhere, the remaining Medjay Elites appeared from the streets. They stood in a line, blocking the city entrance. Walking slowly behind them was

General Kek. Moving past the Elites so that he was standing in front, he was staring Dakarai down. As soon as Dakarai met Kek's gaze, he and his forces stopped dead in their tracks. Looking over at Dakarai, Kek was gritting his teeth.

"I offered you mercy, a chance to escape. And this is how you show gratitude. Today I will not be so charitable. Today you and your friends will die."

Dakarai then stepped forward. Chione quickly tried to reach his hand to stop him. "Dakarai, no."

Glancing back at Chione, Dakarai offered a faint smile. "I'll be fine." As Chione let go, Dakarai then took another five paces towards the general.

"It doesn't have to end like this. You have been blinded by an oppressive regime designed to cause no one to thrive other than the pharaoh. Let us pass so that we may restore freedom to the land."

Kek and the Elites began to laugh at Dakarai's little declaration. "I've known the pharaoh since we were playing together as children. I know better than anyone that he cares for no one other than himself. And yet that doesn't bother me. For you see, you are correct. The pharaoh will be stopped. But not by you. The pharaoh has treated me like his own personal weapon for years, and once you are all dead, it will be my turn to strike back. I am going to rule this empire, and I am going to make some big changes."

Dakarai looked confused, almost blindsided even. Kek was the pharaoh's mercenary, but it seemed the tables were turning. Dakarai was not expecting this.

"Your faith has been blinded."

Kek then stepped forward, raising his blade in the air.

"Maybe. Now are you ready to die?"

As both Dakarai's forces and the Elites took out their weapons, Kek pointed straight at Dakarai.

"No mercy this time. Every single one of them must die."

Glancing back at his forces, although scared, Dakarai knew they were ready. Looking down at Chione, he nodded his head. "Are you ready?"

Chione too, nodded her head. "I will follow you into this and every battle that comes after. I love you."

As Dakarai then smiled at Chione, he glanced back up at General Kek and his Elites. Then, raising his blade in the air, Dakarai began to sprint towards them.

"For the Gods."

As the two forces then collided, their final battle ensued. As their blades clashed, the sound of metal swords crashing into one another could be heard for miles. This fight, though, was considerably different to the massacre at the Nile. Dakarai and his forces were better prepared, and were proving more than a match for Kek and his Elites. However, despite being greatly outnumbered, Kek and his men were ruthless. Still by far the more skilled with a blade, they were continuing to cut down Dakarai's forces. This war was finally reaching its climax.

24
Some Royal Incentive
1340 B.C.

Watching the chaotic scenes unfold from the comfort of his balcony, Akhenaten was savouring each and every sword stroke his Medjay were striking down on Dakarai's followers. His smile grew more and more as each of Dakarai's forces fell one by one.

Back down on the battlefield, despite the continuing depletion of his forces, Dakarai kept on fighting. As Abrax and Bast continued to work together in fending off their attackers, one of the Elites attempted to break them apart by sliding his blade in between them. However, with Bast offering a distraction, Abrax could turn and thrust a long spear straight through the Elite's stomach, causing him to collapse to the floor, dead. Spotting their success, Dakarai cheered, as did others that were stood around them. Their odds were beginning to improve.

"That's it. Keep on fighting."

As the battle raged on, Dakarai and his forces were now growing in confidence and belief. Taking the fight to Kek and his Elites, Dakarai now began to slowly sneak up on another of the Elites that had his back turned on him. Moving right behind him, Dakarai swiftly sliced the soldier's throat with his blade. Another one down. With two of his Elites now dead in quick succession, Kek's frustration was clear for all to see. Spinning his head around in every direction, he tried to work out his next move. Infuriated, he had no other option.

"Fall back. We will take them in the city itself. Fall back."

As he and the two remaining Elites fell back towards safety inside Akhenaten's walls, Dakarai knew this was their chance. He began chasing after them.

"Keep pushing. This is it. We can end this now."

Looking down from his balcony, the pharaoh's sweat was now streaming down his forehead. Glaring down at his retreating general, Akhenaten began to scream.

"Turn and fight you coward. I command you." Turning around, the pharaoh approached one of the Medjay that was guarding the entrance to his chambers. He took a deep breath. "Kek is not to come in here under any circumstances. If he tries to come in here, kill him."

25
Darkness My Ally
1340 B.C.

As Kek continued to flee into the safety of the city, Dakarai and his followers were not far behind. As they all sprinted through the streets and bazaars, the city locals were all hiding away in an effort to escape the carnage. Glancing behind him, Kek could see the mob gaining on him. Still sprinting, he turned to his Elites.

"Distract their forces, but lure the boy to me. I want to end this once and for all."

Obeying their general, the Elites split up and began running down opposite sides of Dakarai's forces. Confused, Dakarai's followers all stopped in their tracks, and began taking the fight to the Elites once more. Fighting in the middle of the chaos, Chione glanced over to see Kek continuing to run away.

"Coward. He's getting away."

Dakarai then looked over to see Kek running. He then clenched his fists. "Stay with the group, Chione. I'm going after him. This ends now."

As Dakarai sprinted off towards General Kek, Chione could only look on in concern. "Be careful, Dakarai."

Turning back to the battle at hand, Chione knew her absolute focus was required here.

With Dakarai now on his tail, Kek turned down into one of the dark backstreets. Dakarai continued to chase after him as the night sky began to blanket over the empire. There were no stars in the sky, causing his vision to be greatly impaired. With his sword in hand, Dakarai slowed down, and began cautiously wandering through the backstreets. His walk was slow and repetitive, with his head continuously darting around, back and forth. Dakarai could not see General Kek, but he could indeed hear him.

"Darkness. One of the greatest allies to a Medjay soldier."

Dakarai's movements became a little more urgent. "Show yourself. Let us end this honourably." With his head turning quicker, Dakarai was darting around every conceivable direction the general could jump out from.

Kek's voice then returned, this time sounding closer. "For you see, in the dark, the victim's heart begins to race. They begin to become sweaty and agitated. Much like you are now. And then at just the right moment, when the victim's senses and judgement become misguided… we strike."

Jumping from out of the shadows, Kek swung his sword towards Dakarai. Just managing to avoid the blade, Dakarai jolted back. With sword in hand, and Kek finally in his vision, Dakarai began to fight back. The booming sound of metal clattering against metal retuned, a sound Dakarai was becoming all too familiar with. Having become considerably more proficient with his sword, Dakarai was able to take the fight to General Kek. However, he was still no match for the leader of the Medjay. After ducking another of Kek's strikes, Dakarai was met with an almighty punch in the face, causing him to collapse to the floor with great force, dropping his weapon. With Dakarai lightly dazed, Kek stood over the young man, with his sword raised high in the air. In Kek's eyes, this was the end.

"Enjoy the afterlife, boy. May the Gods show you mercy."

As Kek's sword swung down onto Dakarai, to his right, he picked up his sword and swung it at Kek's feet. The connection could not have been any more perfect. As he swung across, Dakarai sliced off the top of Kek's big toenail, causing blood to gush out as the general screamed in pain. As Kek began clutching his toe, trying to stop any more blood from squirting out, Dakarai jumped to his feet and began to sprint away. In total agony, but refusing to let the boy escape, Kek began to follow him. Leaving a trail of blood behind him, Kek began to limp after Dakarai; his sword still raised in the air.

As the stalemate continued in the streets, more Medjay soldiers had arrived from their patrols to help fend off Dakarai's forces. Standing firm, led by Chione, their forces continued to push the Medjay back. In the midst of the bloodshed, one of the Elites spotted the young girl that Dakarai had found shelter for. Seeing nothing but another victim, the soldier ran towards the child, thrusting his blade towards her. However, just as his sword came crashing down, Chione, sliding on her knees, passed in between the soldier and child, slicing the Elite's arm clean off. As the soldier fell to his knees, screaming, Chione then jumped to her feet and steered her blade through the heart of the Elite. Another one was dead. Glancing down at the young girl, Chione exhaled deeply.

"Run, little one. Go and hide."

As the young girl ran to hide, Chione surveyed the battlefield, to find her friends, Abrax and Bast were fighting off the final Medjay Elite. Once again working as a team, the two surrounded the soldier, and stabbed their blades into both his chest and back. With the fabled Medjay Elites having been completely vanquished, Chione and their followers could now concentrate on pushing the final Medjay soldiers back into the centre of the capital, and push them back they did. As they all continued to fight, Abrax glanced over at Chione.

"Where has Dakarai gone? And where is Kek?"

Their time had come. The war's pivotal moment had now been reached.

26
The Stairway to Immortality
1340 B.C.

As Dakarai continued to run away from his injured nemesis, he was finally free of the dark backstreets, and had now arrived outside the walls to Akhenaten's home. Dakarai stood outside the pharaoh's palace. Taking a moment to be hypnotised by the scale of this titanic structure, Dakarai was soon awakened from his trance by the sound of his assailant beginning to gain on him. With all the remaining Medjay in the city centre fending off his forces, there was no one to stop Dakarai from entering the palace. Running up towards the palace entrance, Dakarai swiftly opened the door and made his way inside. Just as he did, stepping out from the shadows, General Kek gave a dark grin. He began chuckling to himself.

"I can end them both together. Perfect."

Running through the royal palace hall, Dakarai was desperate not to be seen. To his fortune, the palace appeared completely empty. After taking a moment to catch his breath, the young Egyptian began to hear the heavy breathing of his enemy. Turning around, Dakarai watched as Kek limped into the royal hall, leaving a trail of blood behind him. Glancing over at Dakarai, Kek raised his blade.

"Those who live in this palace are considered Gods. But for you, it is the place where you will die."

Dakarai too, raised his sword. "Not this time. Your days of slaughtering are over. For today you will die."

As the two rivals approached one another to finally end their conflict, a group of the pharaoh's dedicated guard, stormed down the spiral staircase in the centre of the hall. Jumping behind it so to hide himself, Dakarai was out of sight. As the soldiers all stood in a line, they each faced General Kek. The soldier in the centre stepped forward.

"General Kek. We have specific orders not to allow you inside this palace, and near the pharaoh."

Limping towards the soldiers, Kek could not believe such an insult. "I am your general, and I will go where I please."

The soldiers then stepped forward, all clutching their blades. "If you do not obey, we have orders to kill you."

With Dakarai still hidden, Kek too, clenched his blade and began gritting his teeth. "Well, if that is the pharaoh's will, then so be it."

As the group of soldiers ran towards Kek, the limping general raised his blade in the air, and made his way towards them. Despite his injuries, Kek held his own, repelling each and every strike made by the protecting Medjay. As their battle raged throughout the royal hall, Dakarai, still hidden behind the staircase, slowly and cautiously made his way up. With the soldiers distracted, Dakarai was able to make his way up the spiral staircase with no confrontation. He was at last about to meet his true nemesis. As he battled through the soldiers in the royal hall, out of the corner of his eye, Kek watched as Dakarai reached the top of the staircase. Gritting his teeth, the fight against the soldiers intensified.

As he reached the top, Dakarai paused for a moment. With a seemingly catatonic, yet totally focused look on his face, his journey had reached its climax. He stood outside the chambers of the man who took everything from him. Behind this large entrance with a long, red sheet covering it, was Dakarai's destiny. Standing outside, the young man clenched his fists, took a deep breath, and then walked inside.

27
The Thoughtful, the Vengeful and the Frightful
1340 B.C.

As he slowly walked into the pharaoh's chambers, Dakarai looked around, waiting for the pharaoh to emerge. After scanning the perimeter of the room, he suddenly stopped. As he looked over towards the back of the room, he could finally see his enemy sat before him. The pharaoh's back was turned. Having anticipated Dakarai's arrival, without even turning around, Akhenaten knew exactly who had entered his chambers.

"You know, when my father died, I was devastated. I was honoured that my time had finally come to rule the empire, but that could not replace the fact that I had lost the one person who I considered to be most dear."

As Dakarai slowly began to make his way over towards the pharaoh, Akhenaten turned around, so as to face his challenger.

"Now, I know that I have taken a great deal from you. Don't think of it as a punishment. I am allowing you to be reborn. When my father died it allowed me to become the pharaoh that I am today. Now that your parents are dead, you can do the same. Think of this as a gift from your generous pharaoh."

As his eyes widened and he began to grit his teeth, Dakarai continued to walk towards the pharaoh, with his clenched fists causing the veins to pop out of his forearms. With his expression obvious, Dakarai was now feeling nothing other than anger and adrenaline. Stopping just a metre away from Akhenaten, Dakarai raised his blade.

"You kill countless families, and you call it reward. You have no regret for your actions. You are a monster, and you will be stopped."

Unmoved by Dakarai's declaration, the pharaoh simply chuckled. "By you?"

The young man nodded, without so much as blinking. "Yes."

As Dakarai's blade was raised, Akhenaten pulled out his long, golden blade from out under his robe. As he too, raised it in the air, the two of them leant back to strike one another. Just before they could lunge forward towards each other, a small dagger came flying through the air, striking the back wall of the chambers. As both Dakarai and the pharaoh looked over to the entrance of the chambers, they both looked on stunned as an old friend came limping inside. With a trail of blood following him, General Kek had joined the final battle. Covered in blood, but still clenching his blade, Kek began laughing. He looked over at Akhenaten.

"You really thought they could stop me from

getting to you? How naive."

As the pharaoh's eyes widened, Kek moved towards his two rivals. Now all standing close, raising their blades, they were all mobilised, ready for the final battle. Glancing at both his victims, Kek spat a mouthful of blood onto the floor. "At last. This ends now. You will both die by my hands. A new era will befall the empire."

Turning to his former general, Akhenaten glared at what was no more than a traitor to his kingdom.

"You traitor. You dare betray the family that took you in and made you general?"

Twitching with rage, Kek spat out some more blood onto the floor. He smiled at his former Pharaoh. "Your time is over. You call yourself a strong leader, yet it is I who ensures that order is maintained. You hide behind the title of God, but I am afraid, Amenhotep, that you are nothing more than a coward, and today you will die."

Having heard enough, the pharaoh lunged towards Kek, waving his golden blade in the air. Despite his injuries, Kek's abilities with a sword were still formidable. As the two former allies engaged in a vicious battle, the all too familiar sound of blades crashing against each other had returned to haunt Dakarai once more. For this brief moment, Dakarai had no need to engage in the fight. Perhaps his two enemies could destroy each other.

As their clash continued, Kek thrust himself

forward, head-butting Akhenaten. With his giant frame providing the force, the impact was so severe that it caused the pharaoh to fall to his knees in a daze. With one of his enemies currently subdued, Kek then turned to his original assailant, Dakarai.

"You too, boy. You will meet the same ending as him."

Kek lunged towards the younger man. With no time to think, Dakarai swiftly raised his blade in the air, meeting Kek's fearsome strike. As the two engaged in a battle of their own, unbeknownst to either of them, on the far side of the room, Akhenaten was making his way to his feet. Picking up his dropped weapon, he strode forward, re-joining the fight. The three of them were now all engaged in their final titanic clash. As Dakarai offered a great thrust of his sword towards the general, Kek just managed to jolt back, evading the blade. Being the fitter man, the pharaoh was proving to be the most agile. Repetitively swinging his blade towards Kek, his strikes were relentless. Initially able to hold his own, Kek began to tire. With one final stroke of his weapon, Akhenaten slid his blade straight down Kek's left cheek. Jolting back and screaming in pain, Kek covered his face in an attempt to stop the blood pouring down his cheeks. For the first time, the great general was there for the taking. With his rival unable to fight, the pharaoh raised his blade and steered it straight through Kek's stomach. Twisting the weapon so that it dug deeper into the general's body, Akhenaten wanted to ensure that this was the killer blow. As Kek fell to his knees, he began spitting up more blood. Staring on, Dakarai did not speak, his stunned expression offered the only evidence as to his thoughts. As Kek's breaths became both shorter and lighter, the pharaoh leant down so to whisper into his ear.

"I am a God. My name is Akhenaten."

With blood now pouring out from Kek's stomach, his body collapsed to the floor. His final breaths were now upon him. Looking down, smiling at his sinister handiwork, the pharaoh turned around and faced Dakarai. Their war was nearing its end.

"This is my empire, and no one is going to take it from me. I am your deity, and now you will feel my wrath."

Clenching his fists, Dakarai simply glared at his enemy. It was time for one final act of defiance against this tyrannical regime. "You have even turned your own followers against you. You are no God. You are nothing more than a power-hungry ruler, blinded by his own self-indulgence. Today your reign will end. Today, freedom will be restored."

With their verbal warfare having ended, both the pharaoh and Dakarai ran towards one another, desperate to land the decisive blow. Once again, Akhenaten was by far the more agile with his blade, but Dakarai, being the younger man, was showing great agility of his own. Able to dodge all of the pharaoh's strikes, Dakarai was waiting for his moment. As Akhenaten at last began to tire, Dakarai could finally go on the offensive. Aiming for the pharaoh's heart, it was now the young fisherman who was going for the kill. As the two of them continued their epic tussle, they both swung their weapons towards one another at the same time. The two blades collided with such force, that both men were jolted back, falling to the floor. The sound alone of these steel blades clashing was enough to crack the glass objects and vases that decorated the pharaoh's chambers.

The first to his feet, Dakarai picked up his blade and glanced across the room to see Akhenaten doing the same. Taking deep, heavy breaths, the pharaoh had one last declaration to make.

"It's over, boy. Your rebellion will die, and you along with it."

Both tired and injured from battle, the two men limped towards one another. They were both prepared to lay everything on the line for the cause they believed in. As Dakarai continued to limp towards the man that had made his life a living hell, just out of the corner of his eye he spotted something. Movement. Beginning to show signs of life towards the back of the chambers was General Kek. Showing very faint movement, but movement nonetheless, Dakarai watched as Kek's arm began to very slowly move across the floor. Looking back into the eyes of the pharaoh, Dakarai clenched his blade tighter.

"No. Freedom will return to the land, sooner than

you think. Even if you defeat us, eventually others will gain the strength to rise again. You will fall, and your regime along with it."

Wiping the sweat and blood from his forehead, Akhenaten began laughing at Dakarai. The young boy's optimism was nothing but amusement for him. "Have I not made myself clear to you, boy? I am immortal. I am a God. My name is Akhenaten."

With his blade clenched, the pharaoh slowly moved towards Dakarai. This was the end.

But now back to his feet, sneaking up behind him, was his former ally, his former friend. Thrusting his blade forward, General Kek steered his weapon straight through Akhenaten's back. Just like the pharaoh, he too twisted and turned the blade so that it sank deeper into its victim. With blood spewing from the pharaoh's mouth, his eyes widened, and his breathing quickened. Breathing heavily himself, and using the pharaoh as a means of holding himself up, Kek leant forward so to whisper into the pharaoh's ear.

"Your time is over. May the Gods show you mercy."

As Kek ripped his blade from the pharaoh's body, Akhenaten collapsed to the ground. With a stunned expression of a young fisherman, being the final thing he would see, his eyes grew heavy and his breathing began to cease. As his eyes closed fully, Dakarai watched on not with satisfaction, but with a hint of remorse. The fighting was over. The pharaoh was dead.

Standing opposite him, with blood still spilling out from his mouth, and now using his own blade to aid his balance, Kek looked over at Dakarai. He pointed his finger at the young man's head.

"I'll be waiting in the afterlife, boy."

Just like the pharaoh before him, Kek took his last breath before falling to the floor, dead. The two most powerful men in the land were at last no more. As he stood alone in the chambers, covered in blood, staring down at the two dead bodies before him, Dakarai knew the struggle was over. Simply walking over and picking up the pharaoh's golden blade, he turned around and left the chambers. It was time to spread the word of freedom.

28
A New Chapter
1340 B.C.

As Dakarai limped through the royal hall so to leave the palace, he had to step over the scattered bodies of Medjay soldiers that had earlier been cut down by the late General Kek. As he neared the entrance and in turn neared his freedom, he began to hear a rather peculiar sound, one he had not heard since he was a young boy. Somewhere in the royal hall, there was a baby crying. Tracing it to behind the pharaoh's throne, Dakarai glanced down surprised to see the young prince Tutankhamen, being cradled by his mother, Nefertiti. With tears running down her cheeks and sweat dripping from her forehead, the young queen was in great distress. As Dakarai approached what was left of the royal family, he sighed and sat down next to them, placing his hand over the queen's shoulder.

"I am truly sorry."

As Nefertiti continued to cry, Dakarai took the young prince off of her, cradling him in his arms. The baby's crying suddenly stopped. Handing the young boy back to his mother, Dakarai sat back, as Nefertiti began to compose herself. She wiped the tears from her eyes and took a deep breath.

"What am I supposed to do now? I have no husband, and we have no ruler."

Looking the queen in the eyes, Dakarai knew exactly what needed to be done. "This was a dark time for the land. It had to end. Now, let us usher in a new era. One of freedom and prosperity. Let us welcome the Gods, in their entirety, back into our lives. We need a leader that can restore hope back into the hearts of the people. Be the leader the people deserve." Having said all that was needed, Dakarai made his way to his feet, bowed his head before the queen, and continued to head towards the palace exit. Glancing back at the young man as he left the palace, Nefertiti, with child still cradled in her arms, jumped to her feet.

"Wait."

Stopping in his tracks, Dakarai turned around. The queen had but one final question for him.

"Who are you?"

Pausing a moment before answering, this one proved difficult for Dakarai. For in all this time, all this conflict, Dakarai had never stopped and asked that question to himself. After a few moments of thought, after taking a deep breath, and glancing up towards the sky, Dakarai had found his answer.

"Someone who believes."

Dakarai then turned around and left the palace. For he truly was someone that believed.

Back on the streets of Akhetaten, Dakarai's forces

were still battling the final Medjay soldiers that had joined the fight. Continuing to fight alongside Abrax and Bast, Chione was leading the fight valiantly. As the battle raged on, Abrax glanced into the distance to see a figure walking slowly towards them. Puzzled, he pointed towards it.

"Look!"

Many members of Dakarai's forces followed Abrax's finger. Even some of the Medjay did the same. As the figure came closer, everyone was able to make out who it was. It was Dakarai, limping and covered in blood. As he continued to approach, a single tear fell down Chione's cheek. Just by the young man's presence alone, the entire battlefield had now ceased fighting, and were all, instead, looking on at the hero approaching them. Stopping no more than five metres away from the masses, Dakarai dropped the pharaoh's blade to the ground. There was now absolute silence.

"The pharaoh and General Kek are dead. The battle is over. Your ruler is no more, and the regime dies with him. We've no need to fight anymore."

The remaining Medjay began glancing around at one another, unsure what to make of the news. Dakarai then pointed over to the royal palace.

"In there is your new pharaoh. I suggest you go and see to her. It is time for a new era to sweep the empire. Freedom has returned to the land."

After looking at first slightly catatonic at what they

had been told, the Medjay dropped their weapons in unison, then began to make their way towards the palace. As Dakarai's followers dropped their weapons also, they began to cheer, turning to each other, hugging and kissing. As Chione dropped her blade, she sprinted towards Dakarai, throwing her arms around him. The two then kissed, sharing perhaps the most intimate embrace that Dakarai had received in his entire life. Holding each other tightly, Chione glanced up at Dakarai.

"Is it over?"

Dakarai nodded his head. "It is. We are free."

As Chione clutched her lover even tighter, Abrax and Bast then approached their two friends. They too, joined in the celebrations. Abrax patted Dakarai on the back.

"What you have done for these people, for all of us, is extraordinary. Thank you, Dakarai."

As a tear rolled down Dakarai's face, he pulled Abrax and Bast in close.

"Without you we would not have achieved the impossible. So thank you both."

Abrax smiled. "Pilis, your parents, they would all be so proud of what you have done, Dakarai."

As more tears began streaming down his face, Dakarai pulled his new family in closer. As they all embraced each other, Bast looked down at Dakarai, somewhat puzzled.

"So, what shall we do now, Dakarai?"

Looking up to the sky, into the heavens, Dakarai smiled. For he knew exactly what to do.

29
Forever Family
1337 B.C.

1337 B.C. Back where he was young and where his legend was created, Dakarai was kneeling down at the Waset river. The same river his father would sail down everyday to catch their fish. As he stared down the river, a tear fell from his face, hitting the water, causing a ripple effect that went on for around two metres. Once it had settled, leaning forward, Dakarai placed his hand in the water, swaying it from left to right. He smiled.

"Don't worry, I'll prepare the nets for the evening."

Hearing his name being called, Dakarai turned around to his now wife, Chione, carrying a small baby girl in her arms. As she approached him, Chione handed the young one over to Dakarai. Standing to his feet, he cradled the baby in his arms, before kissing her on the forehead.

Chione glanced up at him. "Who are you talking to?"

Still staring into his daughter's eyes, Dakarai smiled once more, and kissed his daughter again. "Someone up there in eternity. I'm sure he's watching us right now." Grinning at his daughter, Dakarai pointed to the sky. The baby's eyes followed. "There are some very special people up there, Gamila, and they are going to help me teach you so much." Looking up to the sky once more, Dakarai smiled. For he knew that he was being looked down on, and that he would be well protected by those in the afterlife.

Cradling Gamila in one arm, and taking his wife's hand in the other, the three of them began to wander back towards a large sand dune. Atop the dune, Dakarai watched over his new, but very familiar home. With rebuilt shacks and structures, Waset had never looked better. Being able to share his home with Abrax, Bast, and the rest of his followers, Dakarai's family had never been so large. Clutching his wife's hand tight, and holding his baby daughter, Dakarai looked around at his new home and family, and simply smiled. At last order had been restored. At last, they were free.